GW00585142

Robert James Oliver

HEADHUNTERS HUNTED

Limited Special Edition. No. 23 of 25 Paperbacks

Robert James Oliver or 'Bob' as he is known to his friends and family lives in Farnborough Hampshire along with his wife and daughter. He joined the Royal Navy aged 15. After 7 years of service in the communications branch, he joined a Japanese company in the City of London where he used his skills, learned in the Navy, in a commercial capacity. Over the next 17 years he studied Japanese. Bob then decided to pursue a completely new career in what he still calls 'every schoolboy's dream job' – Demolition. Bob is an accomplished musician, guitarist and songwriter.

To Lyndsey my wonderful niece. I wish I could be there more for you honey. Lots of love - Uncle Bob -

Robert James Oliver

To my ever-supportive wife Lorraine and daughter Olivia and best friends Colin and Glyny.

Robert James Oliver

HEADHUNTERS HUNTED

AUSTIN MACAULEY PUBLISHERS™

LONDON • CAMBRIDGE • NEW YORK • SHARJAH

A CIP catalogue record for this title is available from the British Library.

ISBN 9781528929493 (Paperback)
ISBN 9781528965897 (ePub e-book)

www.austinmacauley.com

First Published (2019)
Austin Macauley Publishers Ltd
25 Canada Square
Canary Wharf
London
E14 5LQ

My sister Mary Oliver always an inspiration and genius helper.

Chapter One

The two heavily armed Dutch trading ships slowly slipped into the calm blue water bay and dropped anchor within hailing distance of each other. The respective ships' companies began to put away the large canvas sails and set about their new routines.

Both ships showed the signs of recent battle fatigue; indeed it had been a long and arduous journey and now they had reached their intended destination, well, almost the intended one.

Captain Johan Radeur, leader of the expedition, picked up his brass telescope and looked over at the land that he had first seen six years earlier, as a junior officer on a similar trip.

The small sandy beach, sandwiched between a never-ending shoreline of rocks and steep cliffs, gave him the same nervous feeling as before, a mixture of beauty and danger. He spotted signs of a village beyond the beach, just the tops of some roofs, and six or so fishing boats resting on the sand. No signs of life, however, but his experience told him they knew he was there.

This was Japan in the year 1641. Some years prior to this time, the Shogun leader of the now united country had decided to kick out all foreign trade apart from China, Korea and the Dutch.

Even though they were permitted to visit and trade with Japan, there were still strict restrictions on where they could or couldn't go. Johan guessed that due to high winds pushing against him, he had fallen short of the 'target' of Nagasaki by about 60 miles, and now he had to decide whether to wait for more favourable winds to take him down and around the coast or make contact where he was.

Looking around at his exhausted crew and thinking of the dozen injured sailors down below, he chose the latter. Their sister ship, 'Charity', was in a similar condition to themselves.

The battle with a Portuguese 'trader', twice their size, three weeks earlier, had been an epic contest but won at quite a cost, even so, both ships holds were crammed with the finest Chinese silk.

They deemed themselves as 'Traders', others however, mainly the Portuguese, would look on them as 'Pirates'.

Johan felt a presence behind him which interrupted his deep thoughts.

"Eeeerhnm, Captain."

Johan turned to find his first Lieutenant, dressed from head to foot in what could only be described as 'Utter Pomp', this thoroughly irritating man had been the bane of the voyage. He was English, and Johan had always thought that had he 'run him through' (as he was tempted to do many times) then 'bright blue blood' would flow from the wound. An agreement between his parents and the trading company who employed Johan meant that he had to endure this oaf as his second in command for the best part of a year. It had been a very long year.

"Captain, I insist on being the first ashore."

The feathers on his ridiculous hat bounced up and down as he spoke.

"I don't think that's a very good idea Lieutenant. The local people can be very aggressive." Johan advised, knowing what he knew.

"Nonsense! I know how to deal with natives, ol' boy; nothing that a good bit of English steel can't fix." He replied taping with his finger on his shiny sword.

Johan had appreciated his efforts with his English steel when they had boarded the Portuguese Trading ship, but this was a completely different proposition.

"Okay then, but you must do exactly as I say, Quartermaster, ready the longboat! Take six men with you, Lieutenant, 'no guns', and I would strongly suggest that you keep your sword in its scabbard."

Johan spoke in detail to the small crew about how to behave if they did come across any local inhabitants, the Lieutenant however wasn't listening; he had his own ideas.

Johan watched intently through his telescope at the proceedings. He could still make out the Lieutenant's feathery cap flying around in the wind. Then a chill went down his spine. Ten figures suddenly appeared on the beach as the boat neared.

They seemed to appear from nowhere, each carrying an unsheathed Katana and all dressed from head to foot completely in black, just an eye slit for their vision.

Ninja's. Johan had heard stories about this elusive clan during his previous visit and now he had landed himself and his crew's in the middle of a 'pack of vipers'.

The Lieutenant was first out of the boat leaving the six sailors to pull the boat onto the sandy beach. They didn't pull it very far, however.

"Clever boys," Johan spoke out loud, watching the proceedings from the Quarterdeck of his ship, 'The Batavia'.

The Lieutenant, however, took a few steps up the beach and stood haughtily, hands on hips, awaiting a response from the warriors who were lined up in two rows of five; impassive, unmoving.

"He may be an idiot, but give him his due; he does have spunk." Johan said to his quartermaster, who was also watching the proceedings through a second telescope.

"Aye, sir, he has that."

The standoff continued for a few minutes until another figure appeared on the scene. Clad in beautifully crafted armour and wearing a fearsome looking war mask, the Samurai sat astride a handsome white horse who nudged forward, painfully slowly towards the Pompous Lieutenant who was still striking a highly arrogant pose.

The Samurai stopped his horse only a few yards from the Lieutenant and looked over to the six sailors who were now bowing as low as their backs would allow them as instructed by their Captain.

"BOW, YOU IDIOT!" shouted Johan hopelessly.

The Samurai's eyes then turned to the Lieutenant, and in less than one second, he dismounted his horse, drew his sword and cut off the head of the hapless figure in front of him. The body dropped and the decapitated head fell onto the sand, still clinging on to the ridiculous hat.

The sailors on the beach panicked and began to push their boat out to sea.

Two Ninjas lifted their swords and began to run towards the crew.

"Yame!" – Stop – the Samurai ordered, allowing the sailors to make their escape.

Johan was shocked, not surprised but very upset by the proceedings. His main thought at that time was, *My God, he does have red blood after all*.

"ORDERS, SIR?" shouted the quartermaster equally in a state of shock and rage.

Johan took a last look to make sure his sailors were safely on their way back to the ship then turned to his quartermaster and quietly ordered.

"Run out the guns; hail 'Charity' to do the same, but only fire on my orders; I cannot afford any mistakes."

"Aye, sir."

"Request Captain Willis to join us; I must explain to him my intentions personally."

"Aye, sir."

The 'Batavia' was anchored 200 yards away from the beach, starboard side on which would facilitate a six cannon broadside.

The crew rushed to load the 8 lb. cannon while the Samurai and his Ninja guards remained motionless on the beach.

"ALL GUNS LAID ON, SIR," advised Stephan, the head gunner.

"Okay, listen carefully, Stephan, I want you to put a dozen balls into the rocks left and right of the beach, this is just a 'show of force', do not, under any circumstances, kill the Samurai, on all our heads be it, literally."

The surprised gunner nodded in confusion.

"If that's what you want, sir."

"That's what I want."

The 'Batavia' rained down a fierce barrage either side of the small inlet, rocks and tall trees growing on the rising ground exploded into pieces.

The Ninjas formed a protective ring around their leader; one shot went slightly astray and obliterated three of the nearby fishing boats showering the group with wooden splinters, but they remained unmoved, even the horse.

"CEASE FIRING!" Johan ordered.

The acrid smoke cleared from around the ship, and Johan requested a small package be brought up from the hold. Meanwhile, Captain Brun Willis of their sister ship, 'Charity', arrived on deck. Johan and Brun greeted themselves as old friends and stepped into Johan's cabin for a private meeting.

Ten minutes later they were back on deck both taking a long look at the deadly beach. The Ninja's had reverted back to their original position of two rows of five flanking their leader who stood one hand holding the horse and the other a blood stained Katana.

"Orders, sir?"

"Captain Willis will take command from here on. If for any reason I do not return, it has been a great pleasure sailing with you, Joseph," Johan said directly to his quartermaster, using his Christian name for the first time in a year.

The quartermaster came abruptly to attention and saluted, before softening his stance and held out his hand.

"You take care, Johan."

Johan, holding the precious package, climbed down the rough boarding ladder into the longboat that had just returned from the shore. He was unarmed. He would only wear his sword for battle but on this occasion his greatest weapon was going to be his own mind.

"Sorry lads, we're going in again," he ordered the small crew, causing a look of horror on all their faces even though they trusted their captain with their lives.

The small boat headed back towards the beach in the calm sea and when it was a few yards from shore, Johan stepped into the sea and wadded the remaining distance to the sandy shoreline. His grateful crew rowed a small distance out to sea and stood off watching the proceedings.

A nervous Johan walked directly towards the Samurai trying not to make eye contact and walked slowly past the grisly remains of the Lieutenant. He then stopped short of what he imagined to be the warrior's sword swing.

Bowing as low as possible and holding the package before him, he announced loudly in what he hoped would be his best Japanese.

"HAJIMEMASHITE." – *This is the beginning.*

"DOZO YOURISHIKU ONEGAI SHIMASU." – *Please accept me.*

"JOHAN LAEDA." – *I am Johan Radeur.*

On his previous visit, a Japanese translator had explained to him the difficulty Japanese people had distinguishing between 'R's and 'L's, there wasn't a dedicated pronunciation for the sound 'Ray', therefore, 'Lae' was the closest it could get.

After a few tense seconds that seemed like hours, Johan heard a small rubbing sound, the Samurai was cleaning the blood from his blade with a piece of white cloth, then the swish sound of a sword being returned to its scabbard.

"TANAKA."

Great relief flowed through Johan's veins, the Samurai had given his name.

Only then did Johan dare to stand upright and look at the warrior. What a magnificent sight he thought, an unusual height for a 'Nippon Gin' – Japanese person, probably five feet ten inches, more or less the same as himself.

In his experience, the Japanese men were either very small or very, very, large, not much in between. All the women were short.

The lacquered armour shone in the sun, it was mostly black, the signature colour of the Ninja. Johan thought he must have been honoured with a high-ranking official, in fact, this was 'Lord Tanaka', head of all the Ninja.

The warrior gave the slightest of nods, another form of acceptance.

Johan undid the string of the paper wrapped package to reveal a sample of fine China silk to which Lord Tanaka gently ran his hand over, as well as being a canny leader, he was also a fine businessman and knew well the value of this commodity.

"Kiri na," – *beautiful*, he said softly.

Pointing to the ships Lord Tanaka asked, "Fune no naka dewa takusan ga arimasu ka" – *Do you have a lot of silk in your ships*

Johan knew that the word 'takusan; meant 'a lot', and nodded seriously as he repeated, "Takusan."

Johan had been struggling to remember the smattering of Japanese he had picked up on his previous voyage, he knew how dangerous the language could be if used incorrectly, as lethal as the man standing in front of him, so he decided to only speak when spoken to if he possibly could.

"Laeda san wa doshite imasu?" Lord Tanaka asked which Johan correctly guessed to mean *what are you doing here?*

Johan replied in broken Japanese/Dutch.

"Ano 'Big' Kaze, aahh Nagasaki aahh here, iru'," Johan explained pointing to the East and then down at the sand.

The warrior understood 'Kaze – *wind* and of course Nagasaki, Johan's original target.

On my ships – fune takusan men/hito itai.

I have a lot of injured men on my ships.

Lord Tanaka nodded in understanding.

Unbeknown to Johan, Lord Tanaka's mind was working quickly and had been doing so throughout the barrage from the 'Batavia', indeed he had been impressed with the 'show of force' and now he decided to offer the hand of friendship to the 'Gaigin' – *foreigners.*

Only then did Johan notice the difference on the beach, the ten Ninja had disappeared, replaced by a large group of villagers pulling two carts laden with food and a large barrel of, what he guessed would be fresh water, this alone would be a godsend to his crews, their own supply being pretty rank after their long journey.

Lord Tanaka indicated to Johan

"Tabemono mo mizu desu." – *Food and water.*

He then pointed towards Johan's ships and spoke again in simple Japanese to be understood.

"Ano Fune no hito, kite." – *People on the ships, come.*

Johan bowed low again. "Domo Tanaka Sama Domo." – *Thank you.*

This impressed the warrior, Johan had used the correct term for his position.

'Tanaka san' – Mr Tanaka would have been an insulting understatement as opposed to 'Tanaka Sama' meaning 'Lord Tanaka'.

Lord Tanaka did not want Johan to take the supplies and run off. Equally, Johan did not want his ships overrun and due to the fact that Gunner Stephan had blown up half the boats on the shore, this was a comfortable 'standoff'.

"Ei Desu," – *good,* announced the Samurai as he remounted his horse and rode back up the steep beach before disappearing beyond the large rock formation taking the sample of silk with him.

Johan hurried to the water's edge and ordered the boat to return to the ships to bring the wounded men ashore. Before they departed, they gathered the remains of the Lieutenant to be buried at sea. It was the least Johan could do.

"And bring me a change of clothes, my other uniform is in my cabin."

Johan knew the importance of cleanliness to the Japanese and was himself desperate for a hot bath which would be his first in almost one year.

Two months earlier, he had rested his men at a small deserted Island near the mainland of Indonesia which was also a dangerous place for different reasons. The sea was full of large sharks, and some Islands were inhabited by natives that were just as scary as the Samurai, 'Head Hunters'.

His men had discovered a large source of fresh water, a pool supplied by a waterfall. 'Prickly Paradise' Johan called this oasis before ordering the entire crew to bath in shifts guarded by 6 armed sailors. Even the cook had a wash.

Johan turned to the villagers, their smiling faces greeted him, and he bowed towards them, not as low as he had done so for Lord Tanaka but a respectful distance all the same. They were all delighted and returned his bow in abundance, chattering insistently in their strange dialect; too fast for him to understand a word of it.

He then gazed out to sea, now calmed, he had stopped shaking and hoped that it wasn't too obvious to the Samurai that he had been absolutely petrified out of his skin.

He was 28 years old, younger than a lot of his ship's company. He would never entertain the idea of being called handsome, but he was fairly tall, slimly built and most importantly for his current position, blessed with a head of long thick jet, black hair, along with a sparse attempt at the beard. Underneath the hair was his greatest asset, his mind.

The Japanese referred to his countrymen as 'Ginger Barbarians' due to the amount of red haired sailors that had visited their country and many of his crew fitted this description.

As the wounded men arrived on the beach, Johan managed to pluck the word 'Isha' – *Doctor*, from the depths of his memory. The closest any crew member came to this was Anthony, the second gunner, he was an expert at amputations but that was about all. Although impressed, the villagers knew what was required and ushered him out of the way, then began to ferry the sick men away on the same carts that had brought in the food and water. The hospitable Japanese had brought along a huge cooking pot and now a hot fire was heating the contents. Johan remained on the beach reassuring his sailors as they came and went. The greatest assurance to them however was seeing his face – still alive. Only Captain Willis remained onboard the 'Charity' remembering his orders.

"If anything happens to me and our crews, blow the place to hell!"

Johan stayed on the beach for the rest of the morning admiring the organisation of the Japanese taking care of his wounded crew and feeding his men with bowls of rice and cooked meat until, as he was expecting, a higher ranked person arrived to meet him.

Three men approached him on the beach, one wearing a highly coloured Kimono, the two swords thrust into a silk belt indicated his position. – Samurai. His two personal guards were dressed plainly, each carrying a single Katana. He was also an impressive looking sight, an older man short and stocky, but Johan could imagine the strength that was behind the colourful silk. Johan looked at the impassive stares of the two guards but then was surprised at the Samurai's pleasant smile.

"Laeda san?"

"Hai so desu," – *yes,* Johan answered before repeating the honorific greeting process and then stood stunned as the Samurai repeated the phrases back to him ending with "WAKABAYASHI.".

"Domo Wakabayashi Sama," Johan blurted out causing a wry smile to appear on the Samurais face who turned to his two guards.

"Tabun," – *maybe,* and then laughed.

"Wakabayashi 'SAN'," corrected the Samurai.

Johan realised his mistake, there was only one 'Lord' in this town. *My God this is a complicated language,* he thought.

"Kite kudasai," – *Please come with me.*

Wakabayshi beckoned Johan to follow.

Johan picked up his spare clean uniform which interested Wakabayashi.

"Ofuru?" – Bravely Johan asked which caused Wakabayashi's face to light up with surprise.

"Kitanai mo kusai no gaigin wa ofurutai desu ne! Sugoi!"

"Dirty smelly foreigner has requested a bath, how wonderful!"

Roaring with laughter Wakabayashi led the way, Johan found himself flanked by the two guards.

Into the 'Viper's nest', Johan thought to himself.

Walking up the steep incline of the beach and rounding the large rock formation, Johan was amazed to discover that he was at the edge of a sizable town, not the small village that he had expected. He had spotted a few rooftops from the Quarterdeck of 'Batavia', but he surmised that had he been sailing in a lower drafted vessel then this whole place would be hidden from the world.

The town was an organised mixture of shops and work places: blacksmiths, furniture makers, tailors and the like. Everyone bowed towards Wakabayashi and then starred at him, probably the first foreigner any of them had seen. This was indeed a secret place.

They stopped at a crossroad and then after a small discussion with the guards Wakabayashi turned and headed the men up a steep path away from the hustle and bustle of the town. They walked past many wooden houses which were the townsfolk living area Johan thought, trying desperately to remember everything he had seen on his way in, already planning an escape route back to the shore.

At the top of the rise, a large building appeared, a beautifully crafted front adorned the structure. There were tables and chairs set out in an orderly fashion and Wakabayashi immediately sat himself down before barking out orders to one of the guards who hurried into the building.

Settling himself down and prompting Johan to sit opposite, Wakabayashi then ordered loudly,

"O'SAKE! SAMOUKU NO!" – Cold Sake.

Johan vaguely remembered half of this phrase, they were going to drink 'Sake'.

He had never been a great drinker of alcohol but on this occasion, he thought it would be very rude if he didn't partake.

Within moments a small man appeared and presented a tray with a jug and two earthenware bowls. Placing the items carefully on the table he bowed before hurrying off again.

Wakabayashi had decided to 'test' Johan, to maybe see just how much about their culture he knew.

He picked up the jug with his right hand and beckoned to Johan to raise his bowl to be filled. Johan did so with his own right hand, but then he made the grave mistake of picking up the jug with his natural left hand in order to fill Wakabayashi's bowl.

"OEIIIII!" The Samurai shouted, and in an instant Wakabayashi's sword was at Johan's throat and he began to push the tip slowly into his neck.

He quickly remembered something that he had been told,

"If you served sake with your left hand, then your opposite number is obliged to hold his vessel with his right hand – 'sword hand', that left your own 'sword hand' free to 'cut him down'. You only used your right hand to receive or pour sake."

"SUMIMASEN! Please excuse me," Johan blurted out, which stopped the Samurai before he had drawn blood.
Wakabayashi guessed correctly that this young man had never drunk sake in an official manner before.

Johan wished he had learnt more on his last voyage.

Wakabayashi quickly softened, the young man seemed quite innocent he thought, before replacing his Katana with the same 'swish' sound that Johan had heard early on that day.

"Laeda San, wa tsukarimasu ne?" – *You are tired, aren't you?*

That was an understatement, Johan had been awake for the past thirty-six hours and needed this current adventure to stop soon.

"Hai." – *Yes*, that was an easy one for Johan to remember.

"NO MO!" – *Let's drink,* ordered Wakabayashi and Johan needed no prompting this time, he downed the drink in one then held out his bowl for a refill.

"No mo," he repeated. Wakabayashi filled Johan's bowl with sake and as he went to reciprocate, once more Johan made to pick up the jug with his left hand, catching Wakabayashi's angry look, he stopped before correcting himself at the last moment, then poured the drink with the correct hand and a shocked look on his face; it was a gamble.

Wakabashi's frown turned to a smile

"OIE! SUKOSHI JODAN DESU NE!" – *A little joke!* He observed before bursting into laughter.

Johan breathed a sigh of relief before Wakabayashi's sword once again arrived at his throat.

He felt the sharp steel pushing at his skin again and this time feared for his life before the Samurai suddenly giggled and returned his sword to its scabbard.

"Watakushi no sukoshi jodan da ne!" – *That was 'my' little joke!*

The Samurai spoke with a huge smile on his face.

After another two jugs served correctly and a broken Japanese/Dutch conversation with Wakabayashi, basically repeating what he had said to Lord Tanaka, Johan found himself in the arms of the two guards. They were only short but immensely strong, they carried/dragged him along a stone floor and after removing all his clothes, deposited him in a shallow pool of warm water. At first it was warm, then it became hot, then cooled, then warmed again.

Johan didn't care at this time, he was drunk in heaven and he was drunk in hell, but just before he began to sleep, a vision appeared in front of him. A tall, beautiful Japanese girl, he didn't think one existed.

She stood in front of him holding his change of clothing, sniffing at the cloth her nose curled up in disgust.

"Hey, they are my 'clean ones'," he mumbled.

She then looked him up and down. Johan had always tried to be a gentleman, but he certainly was not a prude, he was a Dutchman after all.

If she wants to have a close look, then she can was his last thought before falling into a deep, deep sleep.

Johan was a fairly well 'endowed' young man who would come under the descriptive umbrella of 'Daikon'.

Daikon was actually a vegetable that resembled a large cucumber. Anything less would be termed as 'o'chinka' – *honourably small.*

Outside the building, the tall girl met with two giggling friends.

"Daikon mo o'chinka?" they both asked excitedly.

She shrugged her shoulders before waving the little finger on her left hand.

"O'chinka," she lied.

***

Three figures clung to a cliff face about two-thirds of the way up. It wasn't massive, maybe hundred feet high, but the surface was silky smooth.

Standing back and looking, you would think any climb would be impossible, but there were tiny indentions in the rock that could be used as hand holds, but only if you could hold your own weight by your fingertips.

The first two climbers worked together, giving each other tips on where to go next. All three were dressed in black.

The Sensei followed shouting encouragement.

"Climb faster you idiots; I'm hungry; I need to eat!"

This caused one climber to lose his grip and hung on for a second with just a few fingers. His partner reached out, hanging on with his own one hand and steadied his friend who quickly found another finger hold.

"Dai jobu desu?" – *Are you okay?*

His friend answered with silent 'angry eyes' and they both climbed with new resolution to reach a ledge at the top of the cliff.

The one who had nearly fallen was the first to reach safety and literally pulled his friend up the last few inches of the dangerous climb.

Both laid on their backs congratulating each other but then thought of the 'Sensei' below them; he had not arrived after them as they had expected him to do.

They looked down the sheer face that they had climbed. The sharp rocks below were visible reminders of the danger they had just faced and their thoughts turned to the Sensei, where was he? Had he fallen?

"Nani o sagashite?" – *What are you searching for?*

A voice from behind them asked.

"How do you do that?" asked the young man who had nearly fallen to his death minutes earlier.

"Himitsu desu," – *It's a secret,* the old Sensei replied with a smile on his face.

"Oh wonderful," the other young man announced, "we die because the teacher that has been teaching us will not teach us because it's a secret!"

The old man reached his hand over and gently flicked the boy's ear, which caused him to momentarily role up in excruciating pain.

"That is also a secret; I cannot tell you all my secrets, because both of you have the brain of a mouse, and you cannot fit all my secrets into that tiny space!"

Tsubouchi Tanaka, 17 years old and son of Lord Tanaka, with his good friend Koichi Saito, 19 years old were entering the last stages of their lifelong 'Ninja training'.

They had just completed 'The climb of death'.

The Ninja were assassins, murderers, who would kill silently for their master, and depending on the circumstances i.e.; politics, money, honour, would determine who their master was.

For the past forty years it had been, and still was the 'Shogun' himself. This man and the one before him had united all Samurai factions across the whole of the Japanese islands. This particular Shogun spent most of his time in 'Shimabara' castle on the outskirts of Nagasaki, where he could keep a good eye on the going and coming of 'Gaigin' who he was most fascinated with. He knew there was a big wide world out there and had witnessed first-hand the 'Power of the West' and desired it for Japan, but not all at once, nothing that would contaminate the purity of his Island country, no religion apart from Shinto, no new ideas, just the status-quo of life in Japan for now, eventually they would become one of the most powerful nations in the world, but in his lifetime his main priority was his own personal wealth. He couldn't help himself, he was a very greedy man.

Lord Tanaka's highly trained men spent their working day in this place. They protected the outside of his castle, his private bodyguards protected him.

He was a canny businessman and saw every bit of 'Silk' that came into the country and every bit of 'Gold' payment that went out.

Lord Tanaka himself had an absolute fortune of wealth anchored 200 yards from his town. He was not going to let it go without a fight, and was already planning for that.

"Obi San, we could have died on that climb." The young Tanaka protested.

"Honto desu." – *Yes of course.*

"Naze?" – *Why?*

"You die and then someone better comes along. If you die, then you have failed; if you live, then you have passed the test; if you have passed the test, then you have just begun living, that is why."

Their 72-year-old Sensei who up until this time they both in secret called 'Old Bastard Monkey' was in fact 'Obi Tanaka', father of Lord Tanaka and grandfather to Tsubouchi who everyone referred to affectionately as 'Tsubo'.

They rested happily until they heard the first *BOOM* in the distance, then another, and another. Koichi and Tsubo at first thought it was thunder, but on a bright sunny day.

Only Obi san had heard this sound before.

"ISOGI – quickly, to the beach, leave your packs."

All three grabbed their Katanas and ran hell for leather towards the beach.

The firing stopped before they reached a vantage point, the top of a rock formation overlooking the sandy beach about quarter of a mile away. Around them were pieces of shattered trees and rocks.

"Tsubo, nani o miru koto ga dekiru?" – *What can you see?*

Tsubo had been blessed with the eyes of an Eagle. Obi san's eyes were beginning to fade with his age.

"Two ships in the bay, a small boat is coming in and oh yes I can see Father and his guard, he is unharmed, there is a body on the beach, looks like Gaigin by his clothes, something must have happened."

"The people in the boat, do they have weapons?"

"Six men rowing, one standing at the front, no, he is not even wearing a sword."

"Chikaku no Taifo desu ka?" – *Any small guns?* Tsubo had never seen a gun first hand before, but he did know what to look for.

"No, nothing Obi san."

"Eii desu." – *Good, let us carry on. Today we begin 'our task'.*

The two young trainees stood proudly before bowing towards Obi san.

Their 'task' was to get into position undetected before assassinating the heavily guarded, 'Lord Tanaka'.

***

Johan awoke after 12 hours of sleep that had been constantly interrupted by nightmares of his recent battle. It was very early morning and he looked around confused and wondering where on earth he was. Slowly the previous day's events came back to him.

He was laid on a thin but extremely comfortable 'futon' mattress. Still completely naked, he looked around for his clothes. One of his fears was to be dressed in traditional Japanese clothing that to him would make him feel he was wearing ladies' clothes.

He spotted two neatly folded piles of clothes, the light blue colour looked familiar. The first was his original change of uniform that had been washed and perfectly ironed. The britches even had a neat crease pressed down the legs, but the other small pile of clothing was a revelation. It was an exact copy of his uniform, but the frilled shirt had been made using fine silk. The clothes he had been wearing for almost the past year had obviously been destroyed. His leather shoes had been cleaned, blackened, and the buckles had been polished.

The gentle sound of running water and the sight of rising steam then caught his attention. A bath eight foot by four foot and ten inches deep had been carved out of solid rock and through it ran water from a 'natural hot spring'. Johan was amazed and took the time to indulge himself once again in the pure hot water, trying to clear his Sake induced headache.

He dressed himself with his own original britches from his change of clothing but then could not resist the temptation to try on 'his new frilled shirt'. It felt so good next to his skin, and he hoped it would impress the person responsible for the item – maybe the tall beautiful Japanese girl?

Removing the romantic 'twiddle twaddle' from his mind, he went back to business.

Opening the sliding door of his room, he was greeted by the impassive stares of his two guards. He bowed slightly and they returned his gesture, but still maintained eye contact.

"Doko?" – *Where?* Johan asked, another word plucked from his memory.

One guard lead and the other walked alongside Johan. Small talk would be pointless he thought, so he kept silent.

They walked through the other half of the town which was more of the same hustle and bustle as before but then they crossed a bridge built into the natural rock high in the air.

Johan looked down amazed. Below him was a 'natural harbour' full of Japanese junks of all shapes and sizes. None of them would match 'Charity' or 'Batavia' for size, but he guessed many of them were capable of 'Sea travel'. He also noticed the entrance to this harbour was a dogleg of high rocky land which would also make it invisible from the sea. The harbour was a sea of activity, ship builders, fishing boats unloading the days catch; vessels being loaded and unloaded. Johan got the whole plan in one, *He wants my silk.*

They carried on up towards what Johan could only describe as 'a small castle' built into the surrounding landscape. This was the home of Lord Tanaka.

The main door opened and two more guards inside flanked the smiling face of Wakabayashi.

"Laeda san!" Wakabayashi greeted him like an old friend then pointed to his own head.

"Atama wa do?" – *How is your head?*

"Atai" – *Painful,* replied Johan pointing to his own.

"Atama wa itai desu ka do! sugoi desu ne!" – *You have a headache, wonderful!*

"Hai Wakabayashi san."

Johan responded and for the first time in a while smiled a happy smile.

Wakabayashi picked up on this and commented,

"Tanoshiku no gaigin ga suki desu" – *I do like a happy foreigner,* before bursting into his customary belly laugh.

Another door opened from inside which wiped the smile from Johan's face to be replaced by shock. It was her, the tall Japanese girl he had seen in a dream.

"Laeda san?" she spoke walking towards him. His lips suddenly became dry and he could only produce a pathetic "Hai". He didn't know whether to bow or curtsy.

"It's alright," she spoke in near perfect Dutch whilst holding out her hand.

"My name is Kyoko, I am Lord Tanaka's daughter."

Johan took her hand with his and was surprised at her firm handshake. He wanted to take her hand and kiss it, but that would have been 'far too French'.

He was a Dutchman, and proud of it.

"Very pleased to meet you Kyoko – san?"

"Yes you can say that," she nodded smiling.

"Your Dutch is excellent, where did you learn how to speak like this?"

"Mostly from the men's drinking shacks in Deshima."

"DESHIMA!" Johan blurted out, had he made land in Nagasaki, this was exactly where he would have been on this day. Deshima was a small area built inside Nagasaki harbour dedicated to the Dutch people, a place where they were allowed to have their own culture. Far removed from where he was at present time, and he also knew that Japanese women were not allowed in this place.

"Well I admit I mostly learned Dutch from an old English man called William Adam's, and occasionally I would dress as a boy to secretly work in the bars to try out my skills."

"I had wondered where that English accent came from."

"And how about you? I hear you can speak a little Japanese, where did you learn?"

"In the drinking shacks of Deshima, but I don't remember you being there."

"You were probably drunk."

"I don't drink alcohol."

"Oh is that the truth?"

"Well only when I have to, it's a 'means to an end', but I really do not like the taste of rum."

"How about Sake?"

"I think I could get used to it; I do actually like the taste, it's sort of earthy, more like food than drink, if you can understand that; whereas, I think rum is a firewater that is just full of madness, so how about you? Why do you speak Dutch anyway?"

"Six years ago my father instructed me to learn the Portuguese language, but then after two years for some reason of his own, he changed my thesis. I had to learn the Dutch language. Maybe it was because our Shogun had thrown the Portuguese and their Jesuit priests out of Japan. Mister Adams was always happy discussing that subject. Obviously at that time you people were still allowed to trade with us, so I was re-instructed to learn your language."

"Which did you find easiest?"

"Portuguese of course, I didn't realise I had to die and then be born again in Amsterdam to be able to speak perfect Dutch."

Johan smiled widely.

"I love the way you speak my language."

"Thank you Laeda san; you are so charming."

"You can call me Johan."

"Now that is easy to pronounce."

"OIEEE," Wakabayashi announced as yet another door opened, and the three of them walked into another room with a huge table in the middle. Johan guessed that this wasn't for dinner. Japanese cuisine is always served sitting down closer to the floor, no, this looked more like 'a War Room'.

Johan walked in nervously and was greeted by Lord Tanaka himself who gave him a short bow first. Johan immediately went for the whole 'big bow' but was stopped by the Lord who simply said, "KEKO DESU," as if to say, *That's OK, don't worry about the formalities*. He then barked an order, and a helper with a long tube of bamboo appeared. Two of them carefully took out the contents and rolled the printed silk out across the table.

It was a huge map of Kyushu the most southern Island of Japan. Johan was transfixed, his whole life was based around maps, and this one was a revelation. He saw instantly where they were and noticed that there were no markings on the location. No Chinese characters marking this town, just a blank outline, and there was the 'dogleg', the entrance to the secret harbour. He was also aware of the fact that the Shogun had outlawed maps of Japan ten years earlier. Lord Tanaka was not supposed to have this, but he did.

Forgetting where he was for a moment, he pointed his finger at the map.

"Watakushi no fune wa aru." – *My ships are here.*

Lord Tanaka looked at him with the same big eyes of his daughter.

"Hai," the simple answer.

Johan could see exactly where his ships were anchored. Lord Tanaka pointed to this location and spoke,

"Kono mizu wa abu nai desu, Kamikaze."

"What my father is trying to say is that your ships are anchored in the exact place where Kubla Khan tried to invade Japan many years ago. On the small beach, two thousand warriors attempted to land but were held off by 30 Samurai in that small space. The bodies piled so high that they could not get through. That night the 'Divine Wind' came and sunk all of the ships. Your vessels are resting above the bones of hundred thousand warriors."

And soon one more, Johan thought to himself. He had also heard this 'true story'. The reason the ships sank was because they were river-going vessels. They sailed over from Korea in calm water, but they had no 'keel', nothing to keep them upright in a storm. He knew that 'his ships' could survive anything thrown at them, but still he kept his peace. This was a dangerous game.

Tanaka then played his hand. The sample of silk was brought to the table; Lord Tanaka indicated towards it and then produced a tiny nugget of pure gold and handed it to Johan. *My God,* he thought, *this little piece is probably worth 60 guilders. Let us have a deal.*

The excited Johan pointed on the map towards his ships and said, "Fune," – *ship,* then pointed to the secret harbour. Lord Tanaka nodded.

Johan knew he could get them in but what then? Would they be prisoners, have all their hard stolen wealth taken from them?

"Ato de," – *afterwards,* Lord Tanaka answered and suddenly produced two tiny replicas of Johan's ships. One ship would sail to Nagasaki, he placed the little model in the port of Nagasaki and put another small gold ingot on the carving. "Sugi de," – *next,* he then placed yet another small ingot on the other ship and steered it out of the harbour onward towards the outside world.

"One for me, and one for my Shogun."

Johan thought, *Good plan, I'll go along with that.*

"My father wants to know when you were expected in Deshima on this occasion."

Johan thought long and hard. Every year two ships leave 'Den Helda' in the spring for what they called 'The spice trade'. Only one was ever expected to return from the adventure and even that was not guaranteed. The journey is at least nine months by sail and due to Johan's careful nature, they were probably six weeks late in arriving, had they reached their intended destination.

The authorities in Deshima would have possibly written them off by this time.

"At this particular moment in time, they probably think that we are lost at sea, we are overdue, but then again, we could arrive there in one month's time, two months' time, it's really quite flexible."

Plundering the 'Spice trade' was not an exact science, finding the fully laden Portuguese trader so soon in the voyage had been a stroke of luck.

Johan remembered the full-blown abuse that he had received when he had been appointed 'head of the expedition'.

"He's too young! An imbecile, he doesn't even drink alcohol." As if that was part of the curriculum.

Kyoko explained the time scale to her father who suggested,

"Laeda san, Could you become next year's adventure? You and your men can stay here with us, I think it would be good for everyone to learn, learn from each other."

Yes, you want to learn how to shoot a gun, Johan thought to himself.

"Hai Tanaka Sama, so desu." – *I agree, but I don't have much choice.*

After the meeting Johan was left alone with Kyoko.

"So which drinking shack did you learn Dutch from?"

"Ah you know, Dirty Dickens, Tulip Flowers, Den Helder des-e-des…" Kyoko struggled to say the word.

"Destiny?"

"Yes, that was it, I always had problem saying that word."

"Say it in Japanese."

"Nate kimasu." – *Future comes.* Something like that.

"What is your nate kimasu?"

Kyoko giggled for a few seconds.

"Oh don't try to impress me, Dutch boy, I know why you're here, you are a greedy Gaigin; you only want what you can take or steal; why else are you here?"

Johan smiled and shrugged his shoulders,

"I don't really know why I'm here. Oh, maybe it sounded like a good idea at the time, Six years ago when I was 'Here', I just had the feeling that I would come back. I would come back and find something, maybe something within myself. You may call me a thief, but we are all thieves; we all steal; everyone is a thief. Even you are a thief; you stole my clothes!"

"They stank and I replaced them with clean ones!"

"They were my clean ones! Here, have the piece of gold your father gave to me."

"Don't you ever try to pay me, Dutch boy!"

Johan held up his hands in surrender, "You win."

"Win what?"

"This argument."

"Are we arguing?"

Wakabayashi whispered into Lord Tanaka's ear from the room next door,

"I think they like each other."

***

Tsubo was upside down, hanging from a large tree as if he was one with the branches.

Koichi was disguised as the trunk of another tree; Obi san was nowhere to be seen.

The guards were expecting the attack. All of them had completed this same exercise during their own special training, and they were not about to let their Master be killed.

They were hunting the boys, and Tsubo felt a great feeling of satisfaction as they came and went from the area around his own hiding place. They were in a small wooded area that backed onto Lord Tanaka's castle. It was early evening as the light began to fade. *Perfect killing time* Tsubo thought. *Make the kill and then disappear into the darkness.*

When the area was clear of guards as Tsubo decided, he could 'hear as well as he could see', he lowered the ordinance down from his hiding place. Three bows and three arrows were all it was.

They would only get one shot each.

Obi san appeared in silence from the bottom of the tree and quickly unwrapped the package.

32

Tsubo climbed down and grasped his weapon. Koichi the same. The three assassins then carefully and silently made their way to their 'killing point'.

They 'danced the dance'.

All three moved silently and in complete 'unison', the timing for their moves had been decided on beforehand. Move – wait, move, wait, three moving as one.

Lord Tanaka was in a patio area of his beautiful Japanese garden. It was his own personal 'Best Place in the World'. Here in this place he could think, plan and also 'create'.

On this occasion he was painting. It was a large piece of work, he had his back to a rocky wall, and the flat bamboo board was probably six feet tall by two feet wide mounted on a wooden easel.

He had been working on the painting for the past 30 minutes mostly using large brushes. Suddenly, satisfied with his work, he turned the painting to reveal a life-size outline of himself with target points in the head and chest.

Standing back a few feet he watched the first arrow run straight through the middle of his head in this picture.

The second arrow hit the picture around the area of the heart, and the third, hit low in the genital area.

Undisturbed, Lord Tanaka walked two steps back to the painting and pointed to the third arrow's proximity.

"ITAI DESU NE!" – *That would hurt!* he shouted.

"Yes, but I wanted you to turn around so I could shoot you in the arse!"

Obi san shouted from the shadows before laughing his old cackly laugh.

***

Johan and Kyoko walked back through the town together, just the two of them. She was certainly in no danger, the bows of the few people they passed explained her position in life. To Johan, She was a 'princess' but everywhere they went the murmurs of "Gaigin, Gaigin" filled his ears.

They walked back to the beach together, having a pleasant conversation on the way. Johan finally turned to Kyoko and bowed.

"Mata ato de?" – *See you later?*

Kyoko giggled before holding out her hand to shake his.

"I'm sure you will, Johan," she answered in Dutch.

Johan walked down the steep incline to the small beach to be greeted by Joseph, his quartermaster. A roar went up from the rest of the crew on the beach who were pretty drunk on Sake. Even so, they were all relived to see him.

Johan shook the hands of his sailors one by one, and it was the third sailor who began the drunken chant, "Nice shirt, sir, nice shirt, sir." When you live with people in a small space, they get to know you intimately.

Johan climbed the ladder onto 'The Charity' to meet with Captain Willis, who was in his cabin half way through a bottle of Jamaican rum.

"Nice shirt, Johan," he observed.

Johan gave him a sharp look before declining a glass of rum.

"I thought you might have started drinking by this time."

Johan didn't bother telling him about his recent sake encounter.

"When this is over Brun, we will have a big drink. Tell me where we are."

Johan explained at length the proposition from Lord Tanaka before asking,

"What is the situation with our crew?"

The 'Charity' and 'Batavia' each held a thirty-man crew, half of which were either badly wounded or sick from their long voyage and recent battle.

"I think we could muster enough men between us for you to take the 'Batavia' on to Nagasaki, and the rest could recuperate here and wait for your return before we sail home, I'm not sure I enjoy the idea of being a guest here for any amount of time," Brun gave his opinion.

Johan agreed, but both ships needed extensive repairs and would have to spend at least a month in Lord Tanaka's private harbour. So they both thought over their next step. After an hour long meeting, Johan requested,

"First things first, Brun, can you bring your bible over to the 'Batavia', we have to conduct a funeral."

***

The canvas-wrapped body slid down the plank of wood and entered the water with a gentle splash. Johan felt sadness at the useless loss of life but then, rules are rules and when you are in such a deadly place as this, it is always better to follow them.

"ALL CREWS CLOSE UP, PREPARE TO BE TOWED."

Johan looked through his telescope at the two approaching sea-going galleys approaching in line astern. Sixteen long oars on each side of each vessel powered them through the still calm sea in perfect unison. 'Charity' was the first to be taken in tow. A grappling hook was thrown and caught the thick rope holding the anchor. A dozen or so Japanese sailors hauled the heavy anchor until it appeared just below the surface of the water. Another line was attached, and the heavy metal beast was fastened to the rear of the galley before the slack on the line was taken in by the crew on the 'Charity'. The ship began to move in the gentle tide before the oarsmen struck up once again and then she was in tow.

Faultless seamanship, Johan thought to himself as the crew on the second galley carried out the same procedure with his ship.

As the 'Batavia' entered the secret harbour, Johan noticed that probably the whole town had turned out to watch the proceedings.

'Charity' had dropped anchor in the middle of the deep-water harbour but when three smaller boats began to push against the side of his ship, he realised that he would have the luxury of being 'tied to a jetty'. He shouted out commands to his crew, carefully retaining his anchor from the galley and eventually a gentle bump and ropes thrown from harbour side ensured they were safely alongside' for the first time since he had left Den Helder. A small problem ensued however. His ship was the biggest vessel to have ever been there, and they didn't have a gangway long enough to reach his upper deck. The angry shouting below him made him think, *I'm sure that won't be for long.*

He looked down to the greeting people and was surprised and delighted to see Kyoko standing together with a small lad.

"Quartermaster, Captain is leaving the ship." Joseph had also noticed the beautiful Japanese girl below and decided to give Johan the whole treatment.

"CAPTAIN LEAVING THE SHIP," he shouted to the crew as they threw over the rough boarding ladder and then all stood to attention. Joseph then blew his ships whistle in respect as Johan climbed down the ladder.

Kyoko and her small friend smiled as Johan approached, suitably impressed.

He greeted her with a handshake and a small bow before turning to her young companion.

"Laeda san, allow me to introduce my younger brother, Tsubouchi Tanaka."

They smiled at each other before exchanging the customary meeting phrase. The young man ended his phrase with, Tsubouchi Tanaka – Tsubo desu – *you can call me 'Tsubo'.*

"Hai Tsubo san, Yorishiku." – *Please accept me again, I like you.*

"Can I leave you alone with my brother? I have to attend to some preparations for tonight's celebration; you have been invited to come. There are facilities in the harbour for washing and cleaning, and your men will be accommodated here if they so wish. I will see you in a few hours." Johan knew not to decline, not that he would if it meant being near her.

"And what does Tsubo want to do?"

"Oh that's easy, he wants to see inside your ship."

Johan tried to explain to Tsubo the danger of his rough ship's ladder and for half a second looked around to see if

36

Kyoko was still there. When he turned again, Tsubo was on the upper deck looking down at him smiling and waving.

Johan reached the upper deck and the ever-present Joseph helped him over the last step.

"Where is he?"

"Where do you think?"

Johan ran down to the gun deck and found Tsubo lovingly caressing one of the eight-pound cannon.

"Omoshiroi?" – *Interesting?*

"Tsubo san?"

Johan asked picking another 'gem' from his memory.

Tsubo just looked up at him and made the sound *BOOM!*

"Hai, Big, Oki, *Boom!*"

Tsubo then asked the question that either he or his father wanted to know,

"Chikaku no Boom?" – *The small guns?*

"Ie, nai arimasen," – *no small guns,* Johan lied.

Hearing this, Joseph hurried to hide the compartment containing their collection of muskets, which had a covering piece of timber that was secured with a padlock, the key of which only Johan held and hoped that Joseph would convey the same message to 'Charity'. Of course he did.

Johan then took Tsubo into the 'hold' to examine the carefully stacked bundles of stolen silk.

Tsubo was really not interested in this at all, and he suddenly became a little claustrophobic. Realising that he was actually 'under water' in the hold of the ship, he ran to the upper deck not liking this foreign world. Although he was already a fearless warrior, Tsubo had an unexplainable fear of deep water.

Johan followed the young man up to the upper deck and found him being sick with Joseph in attendance,

"Get it all out lad, it shouldn't be there in the first place."

"Sumimasen Laeda san." – *Sorry.*

"Mizu desu – water, oyobu nai." – *I cannot swim, water scares me.*

Johan realised in an instant that this 'trained killer' was after all just a young boy.

"Keko desu," – Johan's new phrase that he had recently learned – *'it's okay'*.

Johan took the young man into his cabin and proceeded to show him his pride and joy – his maps of the World. Tsubo found them hard to comprehend until Johan produced a small globe of the world. Tsubo had never seen such a thing, mainly due to the outlawing of maps and such by the Shogun, but began to understand its significance, as Johan explained where Japan was in relation to Holland.

Tsubo appeared interested until his eagle eyes caught hold of another item, Johan's sword.

It was just leant lazily at the end of his bunk.

Tsubo grasped the weapon and pulled it slowly from the scabbard, sniffing the steel as it came out of its home. Tsubo admired the craftsmanship of the curved blade and its sharpness. The dotted specks of dried blood told him that this blade had been used recently.

Tsubo slowly, in respect, returned the sword to the scabbard and then looked at Johan who was at this point reliving the memories of the fight with the Portuguese trading ship.

He had been the first to board the huge vessel and had cut down eight or nine Portuguese sailors in a bloodlust, he hacked and speared, leading all of his crew on their mission until the Portuguese surrendered, mainly because of his own mad antics. He would never ever want to go through that again.

"Laeda san?" said Tsubo, gently tapping at his leg to relieve him from his bad dream.

"Johan, namae wa Johan" – *call me Johan.*

"Hai! Johan san! Tomodachi desu ne." – *We are friends are we not.*

"Tomodachi!" announced Johan.

Tsubo then bowed gracefully.

"Mata ato de, Johan san." – *See you later.*

Tsubo then left the ship the same way as he had come, swiftly and silently.

Johan slept on his bunk for the next few hours; finally catching up on all the sleep that had avoided him in the previous 48 hours. Now he was awake, ready to go.

"QUATERMASTER, READY THE BOAT."

"We don't have to, sir, we are alongside; you can just walk off."

Johan put his hand to his head and apologised to Joseph.

"We have found this for you, sir."

Joseph held out a pristine coat that had belonged to the recently demised Lieutenant; they were roughly the same size, he knew it would fit.

"Buckles and bells, sir,"

Johan put on the coat that was really quite special and made him look like the person he was – a ship's captain. He still declined to wear a hat, however, being vainly proud of his mop of jet-black hair. He also left his sword leaning against the end of his bunk.

Johan was not surprised to find that an extended gangway had been built and was in place allowing him to walk off the ship and down to the jetty.

His two, now familiar, 'minders' appeared to guide him up the hill towards Lord Tanaka's castle. Ravenously hungry, he began to look forward to what he expected to be a selection of Japans finest cuisine.

As the main door opened, he was greeted by the effervescent Wakabayashi.

"Laeda san, o'genki desu ka? Mo tsukaremasu ka?" – *How are you? Are you still tired?*

"Hai genki, nagai no nemashita', domo Wakabayashi san." – *Yes, I'm fine; I had a long sleep, thank you.*

"EI DESU," Wakabayashi boomed before leading him towards yet another large room that seemed full of Samurai dressed in their finest outfits. Johan admired the selection of bright colours, *So this is what the Ninja wear when they are not dressed from head to feet in black.*

All were sitting cross-legged on a huge tatami mat. They formed a circle which Johan compared to the 'Knights of the round table'.

Lord Tanaka was of course the centre of attention, and next to him sat Kyoko, the only woman in the room, who beckoned him to sit in a space next to her.

Before sitting, Johan bowed to all and then separately towards Lord Tanaka, he hoped this would be the correct etiquette. The Lord gave him a short nod in acknowledgment, and he made himself comfortable next to Kyoko.

She was seated on his left, next to him was the oldest man in the congregation by far, who picked over his serge jacket, stroking the brass buttons and then his long black hair, making Johan feel that he was being investigated by the 'touch of a hand'. This was Obi san.

"How are you Johan?" she smiled taking his gaze away from the old man,

"Don't mind my grandfather, he is just saying hello."

"Can I run my fingers over his Kimono?"

"Oh yes you can, but then he would probably kill you, and nobody in the room would know you were dead until you were required to stand up."

Johan looked to the smiling old man and bowed as low as he could in a sitting position.

Obi san reached his arm around and touched Johan for one second in middle of his back with stiff fingers which made him relax for some unknown reason.

Even after receiving this 'Ninja Magic', he retained a nervous knot in his stomach which even his hunger could not take away.

Suddenly Lord Tanaka clapped his hands and the banquet began.

Many servants appeared, and Johan was grateful that the first thing served to him was a bowl of warm sake.

Johan was no stranger to chop sticks, but his slightly shaking hand struggled with the first small course until the warmth of the alcohol began to calm him.

There were 18 courses in all, each small dish causing a fantastic taste explosion in his mouth, even the sashimi – raw fish, he wolfed down with delight.

This didn't go unnoticed by his host. "Laeda san wa Nippon no tabemono ga suki desu ne?" – *You like Japanese food eh!*

Johan answered even before being prompted by Kyoko.

"Totemo oishii Tanaka sama." – *Very tasty*. He was getting quicker.

Lord Tanaka was beginning to like this Gaigin.

As the dinner went on, Johan and Kyoko became engrossed with each other's company. They spoke a mixture of Dutch/Japanese as not to offend anyone by speaking completely in a foreign language. This did not go amiss on the men in the room, they didn't like 'secrets'. Obi san just sat contented.

The delicious meal ended with a bowl of soup to cleanse their palates and everything, bar the bowls of sake, was taken away.

Each bowl was refreshed, and Kyoko stopped Johan as he was about to take another swig of the calming brew.

"Toast," she whispered in Johan's ear.

Lord Tanaka stood with his bowl and the rest of the room followed suite.

He then made a short speech that Johan could barely understand and ended with the shout "Kanpai" – *cheers.*

Everyone, including Johan, sipped their sake and returned the shout, "Kanpai, Kanpai!"

Johan suddenly felt immensely privileged to be where he was witnessing the next proceedings.

The men then formed a line alongside Johan, and the lighted candles in the room somehow dimmed.

Lord Tanaka barked an order and into the room came Tsubo and his young friend Koichi wearing their finest clothes. Each of their silk belts held a single short sword.

Lord Tanaka turned to an aid behind him and picked up a long Katana, this he presented to Koichi who grasped the weapon with two hands, bowing as he did so. Thrusting the sheathed Katana into his silk belt, it slid comfortably alongside his short sword. Bowing once more he took two steps backward and next up was Tsubo. Turning once again to his aid, Lord Tanaka picked up a second Katana. Tsubo stood in front of him as he slowly pulled the sword halfway from its sheath to reveal the markings 'YASHIMI', this was one of the finest swords ever to have been created in Japan. It had belonged to his elder brother who had been cut down in the line of duty. He had been roughly the same height as Tsubo and so the sword would fit him perfectly. Lord Tanaka slid the sword back into its holder and held it in the middle, offering it towards a stunned Tsubouchi Tanaka. He bowed before grasping this precious relic with two hands. Placing it into his silk belt. Lord Tanaka then ordered him to pass him his short sword. Tsubo did so not questioning. The Samurai then took out his own short sword and offered it towards his son. The young man was stunned once more and grasped the short sword that his father had forged himself many years earlier. He placed this equally precious weapon next to the Yashimi, bowed and then stepped back to join Koichi. Shouts of 'OMEDETOU' – congratulations rang out as the proud new Samurais milked in the applause. Tsubo especially, this was his 18th birthday. Lord Tanaka wasn't finished however. "Laeda san," he indicated Johan to stand before him. Shock nearly overcame him as Lord Tanaka held out the short sword that he had taken from Tsubo moments earlier. Johan followed the steps of the two lads before him and bowed while holding out both hands. He took the weapon and slid it into his leather belt, the look of awe on his face must have been clearly visible, and he could barely blurt out the honorific thank you

"DOMO ARIGATO GOSAIMASHITA, TANAKA SAMA."

The Samurai's in the room clapped their hands at his small grasp of their difficult language.

Lord Tanaka smiled satisfied and shouted out the now familiar term

"O'SAKE."

Presentations were over. The party had just begun.

Johan sat back down next to Kyoko who stroked his new gift.

"Hey, look at you, Gaigin, you've been here three days, and you are nearly a Samurai!"

"Kyoko san, I could stay here for twenty years and never own a 'long sword'."

"Don't put yourself down, 'Dutch boy', Nate Kimasu, Oboite." – *Remember*.

"Will you stop calling me 'Dutch boy?'"

"Why? That's what you are."

They carried on bickering, and Wakabayashi indicated this to Lord Tanaka. He already knew, his mind was thinking many years into the future.

At the end of the evening, Johan staggered back to the 'Batavia'. Kyoko had left the party earlier.

He had found himself in a conversation with Tsubo and Koichi, in a mutual congratulation huddle. He had a lot of time and respect for these two boys; he thought to himself. They were young and keen to learn the ways of the Western world so he made a promise that he would teach them.

Wakabayashi was the last to see him off, he grabbed Johan by both shoulders and looked him directly in the eyes. "Oh Genki de, Laeda san." – *You take care*.

Johan climbed the gangway onto the 'Batavia' to be greeted by Joseph and Brun.

"Everything okay, sir?"

"As well as it could be, Joseph." Johan decided at that point to drop the 'Quartermaster' title and just call his loyal shipmate by his Christian name from this point on. He needed all the friends he could get.

Joseph then produced a full bottle of sake.

"Need another of these?"

Johan thought for a second and replied.

"I think I have three glasses in my cabin."

"Let's go then, you can show us your new sword."

"Shut up, you idiot."

***

43

In the great hall of Shimabara Castle, the 'Shogun' sat on his 'throne' alongside him stood Funo the leader of his personal bodyguard. Although the Ninja were his 'protectorate', he would never trust one particular faction and had his own guards who would die for him.

He could also call upon hundreds of thousands of his 'Shogunate army' throughout the whole of Japan, and most of them despised the Ninja.

Lord Tanakas 'army' was tiny in comparison, maybe 300 men at most, but even so they were the most highly trained and polished soldiers in the country, and probably the whole world at this time.

Two small figures entered the huge room. A Chinese captain of a sea going Junk, and a limping 'Gaigin' who had, up until the last couple of months , been Captain of a large Portuguese trading vessel on his way home with a hold crammed full of precious silk.

Johan had sent the survivors of his attack adrift in their own ship's boats before he and his crews removed the bundles of merchandise and sunk the vessel with cannon fire. For their good fortune, the Portuguese survivors had been rescued by the Chinese ship that was also supplying silk to Japan.

The Chinese and Portuguese Captains bowed in unison, they had both been to this country before and they knew their 'manners'. The Shogun was no fool, a highly intelligent man who also spoke Mandarin, the most popular dialect of China, and because of his fascination with 'Gaigin', spoke a smattering of both Portuguese and Dutch.

The Shogun listened to the account from the Chinese Captain and then listened to the story from the Portuguese Captain who explained the amount of bullion that he had been carrying.

"Two Dutch ships crammed with silk he gathered, where were they? They certainly hadn't arrived in Deshima, so where are they now?"

The Shogun dismissed the Chinese Captain and turned to the Portuguese Captain.

"You will be my guest for a while, I wish to talk to you again."

"And my men, are they safe?"

"They will also stay with us, I will have use of them."

The Shogun replied, already formulating a plan.

The Portuguese Captain knew enough not to argue. He was taken away to join his men in a secure location.

The Shogun stood thoughtfully digesting all that he had heard. One name kept coming to his mind – 'TANAKA'. He said this name out loud, and Funo nodded in agreement.

***

Johan awoke on his bunk after another sake induced night's sleep. Brun had insisted on drinking rum, and Johan had gladly given him one of the cases of rum that his trading company had supplied him for his own personal use.

Johan just drunk the sake that Joseph had offered.

"I know you don't drink, 'boy', but I guarantee by the end of your voyage you will be needing this."

Johan remembered this 'advise' given to him by one of the company's managers. He had still to this day never desired rum.

After telling the story Johan requested, "Brun, don't you ever call me 'Boy', I will kill you if you do."

"Johan, inside of you is a wise old man, but you yourself have to admit that you do have 'boyish looks'."

"More sake, boy?" Joseph added to the fun.

"I will kill you both with my new sword!" Johan shouted pulling the sword from its sheath, it was only 10 inches long.

For a moment, the three of them sobered remembering what had happened to the Lieutenant.

Then, as one they all burst into spontaneous laughter.

"Did we bury him with his hat?" Brun asked.

"Feathers and all, sir!" Joseph answered.

Johan attempted to sober the conversation, but on this night any sensible conversation was not going to be had.

"So, do you two old bastards trust me?"

"Yes, boy!" they said as one in jest.

"Whatever I decide, we will do?"

"Yes, boy!"

"Even though my decisions may get us all killed in a most hideous fashion?"

The two older men thought for a split second before answering together.

"Yes, sir," this time they answered in a respectful manner.

Johan attempted to stand for a 'toast', but his legs gave way, and he grabbed his two friends as all three of them disintegrated into another volume of laughter.

The next day began a next chapter in the lives of his crews and ships Wakabayashi arrived with a collection of Japanese craftsmen and they set about assessing the damage to the two ships. 'Charity' had suffered the most during the battle, her sails had been hit by 'chain shot', ripping great holes in the canvas. They would have to be replaced along with most of her rigging.

She had also taken a full 'broadside' from the Portuguese frigate which caused the most casualties on the gun deck.

The 'Batavia' had also taken a pounding but the decision was made to only make her seaworthy and leave all the cosmetic damage, after all, they could not sail barefaced into Deshima without a scratch having been in a battle and carrying a hold full of Portuguese silk.

Two huge floating pontoons were fixed on each side of 'Charity' to facilitate the repairs and to, of course, unload the 'precious cargo'.

Johan and Joseph watched this in anticipation.

"Now we have to trust our host, Joseph."

"Trust in God, sir, anyone else can go to hell," Joseph answered profoundly.

More than two weeks passed before Johan saw Kyoko again.

It was early morning, Johan was languishing in a hot bath in one of the harbour's outhouses. She walked straight into the bathroom causing a couple of Johan's men to quickly cover up in naked embarrassment. She smiled looking down at the undisturbed Johan.

"Get dressed, I have something to show you."

Johan quickly dried himself off and dressed.

They walked up from the harbour no longer getting strange looks from the townsfolk. Johan was becoming a familiar sight.

They walked towards Lord Tanaka's castle but then veered off up a rough track heading out of the town. Johan thought that this must be the main route in and out of this secret place. He was almost correct. One hour later he was gasping for breath and covered in sweat. Kyoko looked her normal perfect self.

"Come on, 'Dutch boy', keep up."

"You people are not humans, you are 'mountain goats'."

He replied after having struggled to climb rugged rock covered hills after the 'path' had somehow disappeared. Eventually, at what seemed like they had reached the other side of the mountain, Johan found himself looking down into a valley that, as far as his eye could see, was covered in wild cherry trees with their blossom in full bloom.

"Sakura," – Cherry blossom Kyoko explained. Our national treasure.

Johan had never seen such a beautiful natural sight on such a scale.

"Worth the climb?" Kyoko asked.

Johan was still quite speechless. He just nodded silently, and she was pleased that he approved, maybe this 'barbarian' was quite cultured after all.

She took him to a flat ridge on the side of the hill where they could rest in comfort, hidden from the rest of the world.

"I thought you were going to show me the road that leads to Nagasaki from this place."

"Yes there is one, it's not far from here, but it's quite a difficult journey, our people do it in two days, it would probably take you about two weeks."

"Believe me, I would prefer to sail there."

"I'm sure you will do that soon Johan."

Her use of his name suddenly brought on a wave of excitement, and he began looking all around.

"Are you okay, 'Dutch boy'?"

He ignored this reference to 'boy'; he was getting quite used to it.

"To be honest with you, I'm expecting a dozen Ninjas to jump out of the shadows and surprise us at any moment."

Kyoko smiled at him.

"Well, I can only assure you that the only Ninja anywhere near this place is me."

"That makes me very happy."

"It should, 'Dutch Man'."

A few hours later they awoke from a short sleep still in each other's arms. Johan sat upright and became a little serious.

"Do you think your father would approve of us?" Johan asked.

"With my father, it's not a case of approval, it's a 'means to an end' as you would say. He is really tired of the fighting, the killing, the corruption, tired of looking over his shoulder, wondering if someone is going to put a blade through his back. He wants something better for Japan, and he wants something better for me and for my children."

"Do you have children?" Johan asked surprised.

Kyoko smiled and patted her belly.

"Not yet," she answered still smiling.

Johan was shocked and delighted at this news. Was he to become a father with this beautiful woman? A husband?

"I would have thought that a beautiful Princess as your self would have had the pick of any Japanese man in this entire country."

Kyoko then sat up and became serious herself.

"Oh but I did, I was married before."

"What happened?"

"He was very fond of Sake, I think that's why my father likes you, you are not the greatest drinker, it's not important to you. To my husband it made him arrogant and full of self-importance. In the beginning, I thought this made him

48

attractive, made him strong, but after a while I saw through his façade."

"So where is he now?"

"Four years ago, we lived in a house in Nagasaki, my father was visiting, and he had an important meeting with the Shogun and some Dutch officials, so he requested me to come along with him. When we returned to the house, I found that he had forced himself onto one of my friends. I found her battered and bruised outside the house and he was drunk and asleep."

"In my country he would have been punished for such a crime. Did your father intervene?"

"Oh no, he didn't have to, I cut his ball's off and he bled to death in the night. His family didn't believe or even wanted to hear the explanation and promised to kill me in revenge. Afterwards, my father moved me back here for my own safety."

Johan was not surprised at this story but slightly deflated, is she just using him? Does she even like him at all?

"That is a very sad story, I can only give my condolences to you and your friend. If there is anything I can do to help you then I will."

"Yes there is one thing Johan san, when you leave my country, you will take me with you."

"When did your father plan this?"

"I think it was when you were blowing apart all the defenceless rocks and trees around him."

***

Thirty Ninja controlled the area around Shimabara castle, they worked around the clock in three shifts. They watched the main routes in and out of the castle that were out of bounds to any living creature baring the local wildlife. Inside the castle, the Shogun's personal guard, who numbered around 50, patrolled the corridors and passages full time. The heads of the two factions met for regular meetings, mainly to avoid any confusion that could have had a deadly result.

49

At this moment in time, Egawa led the Ninja faction, and Funo, the Shoguns personal guard. They could hardly be described as 'friends', far from it. Everyone hated the Ninja, and Egawa longed for the day that he would kill Funo.

The Shogun was well aware of this arrangement and quite enjoyed the 'competitive' element that made sure there was never a sign of complacency.

The castle's 'garrison' could hold a small army of a thousand warriors but up until this time, the Shogun had deemed this a waste of resources. Now, he was putting his private 'seal' on a hand written order that was carefully wrapped and handed to Funo who was instructed to deliver this message in person to its recipient. The wheel was put into motion, things were about to change.

***

In the harbour, the 'Charity' was beginning a huge 'overhaul'. Her main masts had been stripped of canvas and ropes. She just looked like the bare bones of a ship waiting to be dressed.

Johan was happy with this, but it was as if he were juggling with three razor sharp knives.

Lord Tanaka didn't want him to leave 'too soon', Brun and his crews wanted to leave as soon as possible, and he wanted to stay for a while, and continue his association with the woman that he had fallen in love with.

Every so often, now fit members of his crews arrived back on duty, and Johan would insist that they all stopped work, and they would have a welcome-back party for the previously wounded men. Every hour of delay was OK with him and of course Lord Tanaka. Brun and Joseph began to get slightly frustrated at the delays in materials arriving and had noticed the amount of time he was spending having 'Japanese lessons' from the frequent visitor Kyoko.

She was not 'showing' at this time, but she had confided in Johan that she was definitely 'with child'.

Two months later, when the 'Charity' was back to the pristine vessel that had left Den Helder, the storm struck.

It began with a wind, the like of which Johan had never experienced. Even in the sheltered harbour, it ran amok, playing with the anchored vessels.

Johan looked down from the upper deck of the 'Batavia' to see Wakabayashi with a rare worried look on his face.

"Laeda san, oki na kaze kite imasu." – *Big storm is coming.*

Kyoko was with him.

"Johan san, we need to get you and your men to higher ground, everyone, get them up to the town."

Johan's men were gathered on the jetty, Brun and his workers were being quickly ferried away from 'Charity', as the high wind suddenly abated and the 'Batavia' gently moved downward as the entire body of water from the harbour began to slowly recede. A huge flock of seabirds suddenly filled the harbour flying inland.

"TSUNAMI," Wakabayashi shouted.

Johan not only didn't drink much, he didn't use bad language either, until this occasion.

"BUGGER THAT, LETS GET THE SILK OFF!"

The men on the jetty knew the consequences, no silk – no deal.

They raced up the gangway of the slowly sinking ship and set about retrieving their precious cargo. It was a matter of time, minutes even.

Wakabayashi ordered one of his customary guards to run for help from the town. The bundles of silk began to appear on the dock. What seemed like a small army of helpers began carrying the bundles up towards safety.

The 'Batavia' creaked and groaned at the natural abuse.

"Slacken off the ropes!" Johan ordered as she sank lower, eventually resting on the seabed within the harbour.

"Laeda san, isogi," Wakabayashi shouted and Johan was the last to leave his ship, now walking 'up' the steep gangway.

They had managed to retrieve just more than half of their 'plunder' before it became impossible to work any further.

Johan ran with the rest of his men, catching hold of one-half of a bundle carried by Joseph, also one of the last to leave. Even Wakabayashi joined in carrying one of the 100lb packages by himself. He had also seen Kyoko up ahead, guiding the men, she was safe.

Nobody looked back, they were too intent on making the climb up to the town. The 'roar of the 'beast behind them spurred them all on.

Johan looked from the corner of his eye at the bridge leading to Lord Tanaka's castle, only then he knew that they were safe.

Everyone looked down towards the harbour about to witness the unimaginable carnage below them.

The initial surge was probably 70 feet high, it came around the corner of the secret inlet, a sheer wall of water. It then consumed every building/ship that had been there. The 'Charity' was put on its side with one of her pontoons thrown on top of her. The 'Batavia' looked to be in a better condition still being upright but completely waterlogged.

Wakabayashi, grabbed Johan around his shoulder.

"Laeda san no hito ga kyojo desu." – *Your men have a lot of spirit.*

"Mo, Wakabayashi san wa totemo tsuoi desu." – *And you are very strong.*

"Oi, so omoimasu? Gambate iru." – *Oh, do you think so? I try my best* before bursting into his now well-known belly laugh.

It was two days before anyone could safely venture into the harbour area. What greeted Johan was absolute carnage. Well he wanted some more time in this town, he certainly got his wish.

The sea had returned to its previous level, and the 'Batavia' was upright; only low down due to the fact that she was full of water.

"Well at least we know she's watertight."

Joseph observed dryly.

The 'Charity' appeared in a lot worse condition. She laid at a perverse angle, leaning on one of the fixed Pontoons, the other laying up against her side.

"She's still afloat Brun," was all the comfort that Johan could give to his friend.

The two captains stood together and noticed a 'parade of Samurai' coming towards them, headed by Lord Tanaka himself.

"Heads up Brun, here come the main people, you know the drill."

"Oh yea; bow, bow, bow. I think you mean heads down."

His friend said sarcastically.

Johan greeted Lord Tanaka and introduced Brun to him.

"Tanaka Sama, Kore wa Baruno San, Ano Fune no 'Bucho desu'."

Which was the closest Johan could get to explaining that Brun was in charge of 'Charity'.

"Baruno san, Tanaka desu."

Johan looked to his friend who was bowing as low as he could get, maybe in fear. Johan nudged him and said,

"He's just said hello, Brun."

Brun stood upright, took one look at the Samurai chief then reverted to his honorific Bow.

Johan thought he heard him mumble, "I see what you mean."

Lord Tanaka smiled knowingly, he was always a terrifying sight.

Kyoko wasn't here on this occasion so it was up to Johan to translate Lord Tanaka's wishes.

"We will carry on, we will succeed, all of us working together, we will recover; we will recover!"

The chant went on in Japanese and in Dutch.

"We will recover, we will recover!"

Recover they did, but it took months of painful work, not only had the Dutch ships been heavily damaged, so were Tanaka's own private fleet of ships including the two sea going galleys that were responsible for supplying the town with provisions, they had to take precedence.

Johan and Brun's crews worked every day to re-float the 'Batavia'. In secret, they were mostly concerned about the sealed barrels of gunpowder they held on-board both ships. Would they have survived the water logging? Only time would tell.

Wakabayashi was a regular visit to the harbour, checking on the ongoing work and ensuring Johan that the original plan was still in place. Johan had begun to enjoy this man's company, his Japanese had improved quickly mainly due to many 'lessons' he had received from Kyoko.

"Off for another lesson, sir?" Joseph would often observe.

"All in a good cause, Joseph" was always his reply.

Kyoko was indeed quite popular with the crews, after the storm she had gathered a small army of women to clean up the accommodation areas of the harbour. All were amazed with her 'grasp of the Dutch language and were grateful for the immense work she had put into recovering their temporary homes.

Six weeks after the storm, the 'Batavia' was upright in her original position, a lot of her top deck had been removed to assist the 'drying out' procedure, and in secret, Brun had opened up one of the precious barrels and had found dry powder. A few days later, however, this barrel mysteriously disappeared. Johan and Joseph decided that it would not be good etiquette to asked any of the Japanese where it was.

Expecting to see Wakabayashi on the jetty one morning Johan was surprised to walk down his gangway to meet a new Samurai, Egawa san.

Johan did not recognise him from the presentation ceremony that now seemed like ages ago. Egawa was the total opposite of Wakabayashi, a very serious man who seemed to be holding the world on his shoulders but would not explain why.

After formal introductions, Egawa san informed Johan that he had taken over Wakabayashi's duties.

He didn't, however, tell him that Wakabayshi had taken over his position at Shimabara Castle, and that things were not quite as they should be; changes were happening, and it wasn't good for the Ninja.

His regular meetings with Funo, his opposite number at Shimabara, had ceased at Funo's sudden departure, and he had been dealing with a subordinate since; a distinct lack of respect he had thought.

Six weeks later, a hundred warriors appeared lead by Lord Iwashima, head of a clan based in Osaka, more than a hundred miles away from where they were. Loyal to the Shogun, they had arrived on a 'visiting mission', and they were about to take up residence in the Castle.

Egawa had stood alone in front of the approaching hoard and stopped them, asking for their 'rights to enter the Castle', along a narrow road that approached the 'North bridge', built over a deep-water moat that surrounded the castle.

He had not been informed of their arrival and felt duty bound to stop them entering. He had noticed the colours carried by the forward party of warriors, Iwashima. And was surprised at such a small army of men; he knew that this clan could raise an army of five thousand or more.

He ordered the column of men to stop, they were led by twenty warriors on horseback, the rest on foot. Lord Iwashima was in a large rickshaw just behind the main group of riders.

Two riders left the main group and trotted towards Egawa, who remained motionless.

The warriors made the mistake of drawing their swords. They had not even pulled their steel halfway from the scabbards when two war arrows thudded into their upper bodies, one from either side. They dropped from their horses already dead.

Egawa remained unmoved.

Lord Iwashima was not stupid; he knew their power, their ability to ambush. His 100 men were not enough to fight 30 or so Ninja. So he relented to Egawa's interrogation and produced the letter of invite from the 'Shogun'.

As he read the letter, he looked up every split second and finally noticed a familiar face hiding behind Iwashima's guards, Funo!

Egawa allowed them to pass.

Thirty-six hours later, he was discussing this with Lord Tanaka having taken the most direct route to their hidden town.

***

Johan, for all his 'savvy' had not noticed that half the men in the town had suddenly 'disappeared' for some strange reason and had been replaced in the working place by women. They crewed the galley that was to pull the pontoon from the side of the 'Charity'. Egawa was in a small boat observing operations as the ropes went taut as they rowed like demons and pulled the structure away from the side of 'Charity'. A cheer went up as the pontoon flicked backwards before 'Charity' righted herself. Brun, who was commanding the galley and the operation, looked down at his girl crew in admiration before taking a swig of his rum.

Egawa then insisted that all efforts were focused on getting the 'Batavia' ready for her mission. The 'sodden' packages of silk had been removed, they were in no condition to be sold. They were replaced by the bales that had been rescued and to make up the numbers, Lord Tanaka had ordered half of the silk taken from 'Charity' to be loaded, filling the 'Batavia's' hold. They were almost ready to go. Only the goodbyes had to be said.

Johan was on the jetty with Egawa who had softened since their first meeting, and now they were approaching the point of being 'Tomodachi' – *friends.*

Lord Tanaka appeared wearing his finest Samurai clothes, alongside him was Kyoko, looking the most beautiful that Johan had ever seen. Her 'bump' was now clearly visible. It had become obvious to everyone in the town and the ships crews what had happened months earlier, but no one had spoken a single word about it. Apart from Joseph that is.

"You lucky bastard," he had once said.

"Laeda san, Gambatte imasu." – *Good luck, do your best.* Lord Tanaka bowed lowly towards Johan and then turned and walked away. Kyoko was left alone with Johan, thirty or so women were on the jetty with her.

They looked each other in the eyes before Johan began climbing the old ships ladder again.

"There is an easier way," she shouted, referring to the gangway.

"Not for us my love," Johan responded.

***

Brun once again commanded the Japanese galley as they towed the 'Batavia' out of the natural harbour and into open water. As the sails were lowered and the wind engaged, Johan felt reborn. Finally he was in charge again, this is where he belonged. The crew disengaged the ropes from Brun's galley, and Johan ran to wave goodbye.

"See you in 'Prickly Paradise'," Johan shouted, the Indonesian island that they had found perhaps a year earlier. This was their intended meeting place before they made the long Journey home.

Brun just waved his bottle of rum towards Johan, oh yes, they would have a drink then.

"Fair wind, sir, West to East, we should be there in two days," Joseph observed.

Johan looked up at his sails, chain shot scars were everywhere, but they had been cleverly stitched by Japanese tailors; they would hold in a storm. There were two holes in his starboard side gun deck with temporary fixings, and his foremast no longer existed. They looked as if they had been in a battle. He sailed on with the sun behind him and as it set, an amazing purple colour appeared in the sky to the West.

"That's good karma, sir."

"I do hope so, Joseph."

Johan sailed his ship on with confidence, not knowing that they were heading into a trap.

Lord Tanaka knew he was.

He knew everything that had gone on in Shimabara Castle over the past year including the arrival of the Chinese junk with the Portuguese captain and his survivors.

He knew the Shogun and despised him, he also knew Lord Iwashima and respected him. Maybe he could become his 'new master'.

Sometimes he confused himself thinking about the politics of Japan and his want for a better life. It all eventually came down to a single thought. "If they do not like what I feel, I will kill them, all of them."

Dressing himself in his 'war' clothes, a black uniform, and smelling his own stale breath from the headdress he had worn many times in the past, he spoke his own personal mantra, eyes closed, gently bumping the blunt side of his sword against his own forehead. "I will kill them all."

Thirty-six hours later, roughly about the same time as the 'Batavia' was entering the harbour at Nagasaki, he, along with every fighting man from the town, was in the Ninja camp deep in the woods surrounding Shimabara Castle.

He was being briefed by one of his senior men.

Lord Iwashima and more than half of his original hundred guards had left the Castle and were on their way to meet up with the rest of his army which reports said numbered eight hundred or more. Lord Tanaka's men numbered less than three hundred. This would be a 'fair fight', he announced to them all.

***

Johan Sailed into Nagasaki harbour, a familiar sight. Deshima was on his right and as he dropped sail two large sea boats approached to push the 'Batavia' alongside the jetty.

There were no other foreign vessels in the harbour. Just him and he was waiting for a shout from another Dutch person, it never happened. As the 'Batavia' was pushed alongside the jetty a 'welcoming party' of Shogun guards appeared.

Johan decided to only speak in Dutch; something was amiss.

Japanese workers pushed a gangway onto the 'Batavia' and he was the first to leave his ship.

He was greeted with swords aimed at his throat by two warriors and urged to follow them.

The rest of the crew were ushered from the ship and imprisoned in a nearby building. A thorough search of the ship was made before a gang of workers removed the precious silk from the cargo hold.

Johan was taken to a separate room and tied to a chair, the door was locked behind them and three men dressed in light clothing began their interrogation.

"Namae wa?" – *What is your name?*

Even before he could speak, a hand slashed him across his face.

"Namae wa?" The beating went on relentlessly until both sides of his face were broken, and he was unconscious. Even his sparse beard offered no defence against this sort of abuse.

"Namae wa?" Even though he wanted to say his name, they would not let him and this process went on for hours and hours.

When eventually the beating stopped, Johan looked to see the Portuguese Captain of the ship that he had 'plundered' standing in front of him.

"I thank you so much Captain, you have brought 'my cargo' back to me, and now I will take your ship from you, shall I show you my payment?."

The Portuguese Captain held a box of gold that he could barely lift, opened the lid and shouted into Johan's face,

"There you go you 'English Bastard'."

Johan saw the irony of this statement.

"You are going to die, and I am going home in your ship with this."

Johan could not even mumble a reply.

***

The Portuguese Captain walked triumphantly up the gangway of the 'Batavia' leading his men and shouting orders; he wanted to set sail as soon as possible.

Four of his men went aloft to set the main sail's, they worked for a while before becoming silent.

Four decapitated heads then dropped to the upper deck from the masts followed quickly by four bodies.

Oh my God, the Portuguese captain thought, *are we ever going to get out of this hellhole?*

Koichi Saito had remained hidden on the 'Batavia' since they sailed under instruction from Lord Tanaka, he did not want his grandchild to be without a father.

The ghostly figure dressed in black slid down one of the main sheets and set about the rest of the Portuguese crew who ran for the safety of the dock as quickly as they could.

The Captain appeared, struggling with the heavy box of gold, and Koichi beckoned him back to the main cabin on the upper deck. He placed the box underneath Johan's bunk just before Koichi killed him

Koichi looked down towards the Jetty, six warriors began edging slowly up the ships gangway. As the first one set foot on the 'Batavia', Koichi appeared from nowhere and sliced him in half, cutting down two others before the remaining three ran for their lives. They would need more men.

Koichi smiled to himself before running down below deck and hiding, he was going to be their 'worst nightmare'.

Johan's torturers threw buckets of cold water over him and began repeating their benign questioning, "Namae wa? Namae wa?"

Through bloodshot eyes, Johan thought he could see the large black key in the door in front of him slowly turn by itself.

"NAMAE WA?"

A voice from behind the three men suddenly announced himself.

"WAKABAYASHI DESU."

They turned around in horror.

He made a small incision into the main protagonist's throat, purposely cutting half way through his windpipe to ensure that he would die the most hideous death, drowning in his own blood. The other two he despatched in a split second slicing through the tops of their heads with two quick blows from his Katana.

Cutting through Johan's bonds, Wakabayashi remarked,

"Laeda san, mo ichi do atama ga itai desu ne." – *Once again you have a sore head.*

There were no limits to this man's dark sense of humour.

Koichi waited patiently in the dark shadows of the Batavia's gun deck.

He heard them coming, he had no idea how many were hunting him, it didn't matter, 'he would kill them all'.

This time it was the Shogun's personal guard leading the attack. Cleverly the warrior in charge instructed his men to open the gun ports so that light entered the area, they moved slowly towards Koichi who was crouched behind the last cannon. Koichi decided at this point to Test out his sword skills.

Koichi stood brazenly in front of the approaching warriors, sword in his scabbard, challenging, and the 'leading warrior' took the bait.

They stood face to face in a tense standoff, the older warrior verses the boy dressed in black.

As the older man drew his sword, Koichi bent his knees and pulled his own into a swift sideways motion. The older man's sword bounced against the low wood work, interrupting his action, and Koichi sliced him with a sideways cut across his belly, and finished him off with a reverse stab to the heart.

Retrieving his sword, he then stood back and removed his Ninja mask before smiling madly towards the rest of his aggressors, there was now no need for secrecy and for his final lack of respect towards them, turned his back. *Oh well*, he thought, *he was enjoying himself.*

Wakabayashi picked up the beaten Johan, outside the cell they met with his two 'shadows'; Johan recognised them even with their Ninja scarfs.

They made their way to where the rest of his men were imprisoned. Two men were on guard, but Wakabayashi's men took care of them in an instant.

They searched the dead guards for the key to the cell, but then Wakabayashi became impatient.

Sizing up the heavy oak door, he took one heavy breath in before smashing through the lock with his left elbow. There was no scream before, no pre build up – just a small output of breath after the event. During battle, the Ninja did not make any unnecessary noise.

Joseph was the first to take over the care of Johan.

Wakabayashi and one of his guards ran off leaving the other to protect the Dutch sailors. They all headed towards the 'Batavia'.

Koichi stood with his back to the warriors head down and listening as they edged forward with swords drawn. They had stopped opening the gun ports, and Koichi stood in the shadows. Two warriors attacked but their cuts fell short due to the bad light, and another Ninja trick, he quickly turned and cut both their sword arms off.

The two bodies writhed around on the deck, blocking the way for any further attack, one tried and Koichi sliced through his shoulder blade, causing him to fall on top of his wounded comrades. The others seemed to give up the fight and retreated only to be met by Wakabayashi and his guard coming up the ships gangway.

A disappointed Koichi despatched the three wounded men at his feet and headed for the upper deck to be met with Wakabayashi, his guard and a pile of dead bodies.

Koichi smiled a psychotic smile before his ear was 'flicked' by Wakabayashi. The same 'punishment that Obi san had administered after their 'climb of death'.

This time, however, he absorbed the pain and instead felt a pang of anger before controlling himself and re-addressing his headscarf.

Wakabayashi gave the young man a sharp second look before shouting towards Johan.

"LAEDA SAN ISOGI, ITE! ITE!" – *Quickly, you must go.*

Joseph and the crew did not need a second telling, they hurried like madmen, throwing the many bodies from the ship and hurrying to lower their sails. Johan was taken to his cabin and laid on his bunk. Wakabayashi looked up towards Joseph, who nodded and then cut through the heavy ropes anchoring the ship to the harbour with his sword. As the 'Batavia' edged away from the harbour wall, the gangway dropped into the water.

Joseph took his last look towards the jetty, wanting to wave goodbye to Wakabayashi and his men but they were gone.

The 'Batavia' moved painfully slowly away from the Deshima harbour wall and then a breath of wind from God blew them away from danger.

Only when they reached open sea, Joseph relaxed and visited Johan in his cabin.

"How are you, sir?"

"Could be better Joseph," he barely managed to mumble.

"Did you give all that rum to Brun?"

Johan pointed to the underneath of his bunk.

Joseph rummaged around underneath Johan's bunk and found the rum.

Swigging a large gulp he then took a handful of the liquid and rubbed it into Johan's broken face.

Johan reeled in pain, but alcohol was a good tonic for his condition.

"That's not the only thing that's under your bunk, sir." Joseph smiled before taking another large mouthful.

***

Kyoko and Obi san were with Brun on the deck of the 'Charity' talking about Johan, the grandfather listened intently at Kyoko's interpretation of Johan, although he had found out everything he needed to know from his own investigation. He had done the same thing with Brun, and there was something that he didn't like, but he couldn't quite put his finger on it.

Kyoko was now eight months into child, her bump was proud, Obi san, along with her brother Tsubo were to accompany her to Holland to be her chaperone, her protectorate. Tsubo would join them on his return from Shimabara Castle, if he managed to that was, Lord Tanaka needed every fighting man he could get at this time.

Obi san had been instructed to remain with Kyoko, he was not too old to not want another adventure in his life but secretly happy he was missing this battle.

He was one of the original Ninja that protected the First Shogun in an epic march from 'Kyo' the old Capital to Edo many years earlier. Had they failed then, there would not be a Shogunate in place at this time. Their secret town had been sanctioned by Lord Tokugawa himself and had thrived and grown. Things were different now, the new Shogun was corrupt, greedy and cruel; he wanted everything for himself. Lord Tanaka had now decided to 'Find a new master'.

***

Wakabayashi, his two guards and Koichi hurried to Shimabara Castle.

The main entrance was heavily guarded, it was a wooden bridge over a deep water-filled moat on the South side of the Castle, the only other entrance was a similar bridge on the opposite North side, but of course they knew another way in.

Wakabayashi and his two men took this secret route into the castle but Koichi peeled off against orders and walked straight across the bridge leading to the main entrance confronting the dozen or so guards face to face. Underneath his headscarf he was smiling like a madman.

"Stupid boy!" Wakabayashi shouted silently.

They all charged the young Ninja, and he ran towards them. Just before making contact, Koichi forward somersaulted them all and began attacking from their rear.

Koichi sliced through four of them in the air before they had even turned around. He then rolled into the middle of the pack of warriors and attacked them like a whirlwind. It was all over in a matter of seconds.

Koichi then walked nonchalantly into the castle towards the main hall humming a happy tune and dancing a happy dance; he was having 'fun', and he did not want this moment to end.

The Shogun sat on his 'Kings throne' surrounded by advisors and guards numbering about forty in total.

Wakabayashi and his two men walked brazenly into the hall via a small side door and stood menacingly facing the throng of warriors outnumbered by at least four to one.

"ATTE!" – *hit them*, The Shogun screamed.

Then began the mother of all close quarters battle.

The Ninja fought in a 'triangle formation'. Wakabayashi had wanted a diamond, but Koichi was still sauntering his way towards the hall.

"Where is that dam boy?" Wakabayshi shouted inwardly.

The three Ninja fought hard but were being backed into a corner One of Wakabayashi's men had suffered a serious wound to his upper arm but was still fighting one handed.

The main doors to the hall suddenly burst open. Everyone stopped to look for a split second to see Koichi, minus his headscarf, standing arms aloft holding both of his swords.

"KOICHI SAITO, IMASU!" – *Koichi is here!*

Wakabayashi shook his head before carrying on the fight. He took a serious cut himself just above the knee, and one of his men was cut down before Koichi steamed into action; killing all before him.

The fight ended with bodies everywhere. Wakabayashi and his remaining man were on the floor trying to stem the blood coming from their wounds.

Only Koichi remained standing, completely unscathed, fifteen feet away from the Shogun who had remained seated for the whole of the small battle. He put away both of his swords and stood challenging this most powerful man.

"I suppose I will have to do this by myself," The Shogun said as he grabbed at his sword and made to get up from his throne.

Koichi reached down to his ankle and picked up a throwing knife that he despatched into the heart of the Shogun who slumped back onto his seat.

Koichi approached the dead figure, picked him up from under his arms and threw the body to one side before taking his place on the throne.

Wakabayashi looked at the boy who was smiling madly imagining that he was the new 'King'. Barking out orders to non-existent people, Wakabayashi looked at him worriedly. The boy had lost his mind. He had seen this before.

He and his guard helped each other out of the castle and across the North Bridge, towards the safety of the Ninja position.

Lord Tanaka and Tsubo were underneath this bridge, fixing the barrel of gunpowder taken from the 'Batavia' to the supports of the wooden structure.

He knew a little about the power of the 'black powder' and fixed a long fuse, also taken from Johan's ship, into the dust like substance before sealing the top tightly with small rocks wrapped with ribbons of silk.

Lord Tanaka struck his short sword against a piece of flint causing sparks to ignite the three-foot long lanyard. As it fizzed away, Lord Tanaka ordered, "Tsubo, isogi, ite" – *Let's go quickly.*

They hurried for cover before looking back to watch from a safe area, waiting in expectation.

To their horror, Koichi walked onto the bridge wearing a hat that he had taken from the demised Shogun and holding both of his swords high in the air.

He began to shout –

"KOICHI SA…" *BOOM*!

The whole bridge exploded in a shower of splinters and a cloud of black smoke.

When the explosion died down, Koichi was nowhere to be seen.

Tsubo was shocked, his best friend had disappeared, and he had helped set the charge.

Lord Tanaka noticed this and barked an order towards him, instructing him to arm himself, there was no room for any sentiment at this time. Iwashima's now two thousand warriors were approaching, and the real battle was about to begin.

With the bridge gone, Iwashima's army were now concentrated on the main road heading towards the Castle. Either side of the road were thick wooded areas, perfect Ninja ambush country.

The Ninja's system was based on ambush tactics fought in phases. First team attacked then pulled back, second team attacked them pulled back, third team attacked and pulled back while the first and second teams manoeuvre to 'outflank' the oncoming threat.

The problem was on this occasion, Lord Iwashima was aware of the Ninja's method and he had so many men at his disposal that he could afford to take advantage of the fact.

He would attack on such a large front that the Ninja would not be able to get behind his ranks of men four or five deep.

All of Lord Tanaka's men were gathered on the West side of the road. He did not want to 'split his forces' and in the event of failure, they could safely retreat to the town through such a dangerous route that Iwashima's men could not hope to follow.

Tsubo was with a team of archers with his favourite bow and a sheath crammed full of long war arrows. His skill with a sword was excellent but still not on the level of Koichi who had been off the scale, but with a bow, he was second to none in the town. Ever since he could walk, he could shoot. His father had fashioned him a 'toy' baby bow and within a week, he had killed half the chickens in the town before they removed the sharp tips on his small arrows.

Tsubo was in the first phase of the Ninja at the south side, they would make the first kill.

Iwashima had set up camp at the north end of the woods leading to Shimabara castle.

He knew where the main Ninja camp was; Funo had not been lazy as a Shogun guard. He knew as much about them as they him.

They would attack the whole area as one sweeping brush from the north, south and centre. He mostly desired to capture the area around the North Bridge even though the Ninja had destroyed the structure, and they could not deploy to the Castle. They would have the Ninja pinned into a corner. He kept his mounted warriors in reserve for this purpose.

Everything had to happen at once. Lord Iwashima knew he had to stretch the Ninja resources to win the battle. Lord Tanaka also knew this and he had put his greatest resource at the bridge, his son Tsubo. If they captured that area then the war was lost. It was the foothold of the battle.

Iwashima's army headed down the road, five deep, carrying an array of weapons. Men with spears, bow's and katanas.

Lord Tanaka let them come. There was an area of open ground just before the North Bridge. The first hundred warriors came to a halt there, and after them each body of men stopped until a line of men at least a half of a mile long filled the road.

One loud command went up, and they all turned as one towards the West, weapons at their ready.

Tsubo had observed the proceedings and had not been impressed from where he was. He had at least thirty 'easy' targets to aim for, what a waste of life he thought to himself, knowing that he would be taking theirs soon.

"ATTE," he heard the command in the distance. And then he and his team began to kill everything and everyone in front of them.

After running out of his collection of 30 arrows, he ran back to a rearming point to allow the next 'team' to carry on the work. He passed by a group of fellow Ninja's who were ready with swords: 'the third phase'.

Tsubo replenished his sheath with thirty more arrows then hid in the woods alongside his fellow bowmen.

Lord Tanaka was in the Centre Ninja camp holding himself back, he was the 'main reserve' if all else failed then he would have to fight, and that would not be a pretty sight at all.

The North and Centre groups held their own for a while but then this was a war of attrition. Numbers began to count.

Tsubo and his comrades held the South side until a cavalry of mounted warriors from Iwashima stormed down the road into his position. Their supply of arrows had ran out and they were down to a few men, Tsubo was knocked over by a passing warrior on horseback and now laid unconscious on the ground.

In his dreams Tsubo wished Koichi could be here now, but all of a sudden he was, clothes tattered and his face blackened with gunpowder smoke.

"I'm sorry it's bad, but you have to kill the horses," Koichi advised.

"I can't kill a horse, I love them."

"In which case you have to tell the horse that, before you kill the man."

Tsubo staggered to his feet and ran straight in front of the next warrior on horseback.

"UMA!" – *Horse*, this command stopped the beast in its tracts and threw the passenger from its back, the figure flying over his head.

Tsubo had never seen such a horse before and he instantly wanted to stroke and admire this beautiful animal.

He dearly loved his father's horse but that was the only one in his town, although looking magnificent, it was pretty old and slow. This beast was different, it was young, fit and strong. He patted the creature down its neck. "Oh I would love to have the pleasure of being on your back, and I would be your best friend," he said before sensing danger behind him.

Tsubo then drew his sword and fended of a sword attack from the horse's rider without even bothering to turn around. Still not turning, he stamped his back heal into the opponents shin causing him instant pain, before smashing his face with his elbow through the riders colourful helmet, with such force that the headpiece broke in two and landed on the ground. Only then did he turn around to look at the warrior who seemed to be even younger than himself.

"Namae wa nan desu ka?" – *What is your name?*

Tsubo asked holding his Yashimi to the young man's throat and cutting it slightly until he divulged his information.

"Iwashima desu."

Tsubo was about to kill him but upon hearing this name thought otherwise.

He then replaced his Yashimi before whacking the young warrior on top of his head with his sharp knuckles causing him to become unconscious and then lifted him across the horse's neck. He then leapt on to the animals back and began to make his way to the centre group.

His southern end had lost most of his men had been killed. If this was a relation to Lord Iwashima then the bargaining power would be immense.

Tsubo trotted into the main Ninja camp to be greeted by his father. He threw the young warrior onto the ground who landed in a heap and advised, "Iwashima desu."

"Oh so desu ne? Wakaku no Iwashima desu." – *A young Iwashima eh?*

There now began a lull in the battle, both sides regrouped and gathered their wounded.

Tanaka's men all now converged on the centre area, awaiting the final thrust from Iwashima. Lord Tanaka counted 173 fit men.

Lord Tanaka took his son to one side. His work there was done. There was no point in Tsubo staying for the final part of the battle; he and his Ninja would give him enough time to return to the town and depart with the 'Charity' as previously planned. Tsubo took off his empty arrow sheath and put it to one side with his bow, before embracing his father for the first time since he had been a small boy. Lord Tanaka returned his affections before simply saying,

"Oh genki de, Tsubouchi." – *Take care my son.*

Tsubo mounted his new horse and rode away swiftly, he knew he would have to leave his mount for the last climb towards the town, but still, the journey time would be cut in half. He was sure that the intelligent creature could find his way back to his original owner.

Lord Iwashima had stopped the battle to take stock of the situation. He had lost close on to 400 men, even though he knew he could win the battle, he was sick of the useless slaughter which, as reports went, included his son.

Another report came in, 'The Shogun had been assassinated by the Ninja!'

His clever mind went into overdrive, according to the laws of the land, he was now the most senior Lord in all of Japan.

Funo and five of his remaining men on horseback rode up to Iwashima.

"KILL THEM, WE MUST KILL THEM ALL TO AVENGE THIS!"

Iwashima relaxed and gave the simple order to Funo,

"Ite." – *Go on then*.

He might as well had thrown a knife towards Funo and had him commit 'Seppuku' – ritual suicide.

Funo understood this perfectly well.

He turned his small troop of warriors and headed towards the Ninja position.

As their horses gathered speed, the six men shouted,

"BANZAI, BANZAI!" – *long live the king!*

Then as they rode into the woods, all went silent. Egawa stood finally satisfied, holding a Katana that was dripping with the blood of Funo.

Lord Iwashima sent an unarmed trio of 'envoys' into the woods carrying his flag of office. The forward phase of Ninja allowed them to pass and then the second. Eventually they came face to face with Lord Tanaka.

"We have been told to offer you a peace settlement, if you offer your allegiance to Lord Iwashima, then you can all live, apart from you, Lord Tanaka. Lord Iwashima wishes for you to kill yourself.

You have killed a Shogun, how would my master know that you would not kill him as well?"

Lord Tanaka then produced the young Iwashima.

The envoys talked amongst themselves for a short while before announcing.

"I think we could come to an arrangement."

***

Tsubo rode like he had never done before, the power of the beast underneath him was incredible but then, at the end of the endless cherry tree orchard, he reluctantly stopped and dismounted.

Tsubo removed the saddle and bridle, at least his newfound friend could run fee for a while, then for a second time that day, he said goodbye to a loved one.

As he ran into the town past his father's castle, he suddenly thought about what would happen if the ship was not there? Secretly he was hoping that the ship had gone and he would not have to experience 'deep water'.

His fears retained as he saw the 'Charity' in her full glory, his new world, his future. As he ran down the dock, cheers ran out "TSUBO, TSUBO!"

He climbed into a small boat that took him to the 'Charity' and leapt up the side of the ship even without the help of the ship's ladder.

Kyoko was the first to greet him, and even Obi San grabbed his grandson in a family hug.

"HAUL ANCHOR!" Brun ordered to his team of Japanese women and Dutch men on board.

Because the 'Batavia' needed a full complement of crew, he had been forced to make up the numbers with local girls without marital commitments who had volunteered for a 'new adventure'.

Brun had a chest of Tanaka's gold, similar to the one on the 'Batavia' safely hidden in his cabin. With their newfound wealth, he would create a new 'Deshima' but this time in Amsterdam. With their cooking skills and sense of industry and of course his sharp business brain, they could not fail. Kyoko had been impressed with Brun's ideas and had helped sell the idea to the girls, even beginning to start them off with the basics of the Dutch language.

The Japanese galley, now crewed by older women and older men from the town, picked up the anchor and began the reverse procedure to take the 'Charity' out to the open sea.

As the ship picked up her anchor in the open sea, the shouts from the galley went up.

"GAMBATTE, GAMBATTE!" – *Good luck, do your best!*

'Charity' dropped her sails, and Brun felt the wind take her. For the first time in almost a year he felt truly free, the mouthful of rum he took from his bottle was the sweetest he'd ever tasted.

The 'Batavia' had left Nagasaki a day earlier, and Brun thought briefly about waiting for Johan to catch up but quickly dissuaded this thought. He wanted to be away from this place as quickly as he possibly could, besides, the 'Batavia' was missing a foremast which would considerably slow their progress. No, Brun put on every bit of canvas that was available and made speed.

***

Brun's motley crew of Dutch sailors, some with limbs missing, and Japanese girls performed well over the next three weeks, even Tsubo and Obi san joined in the shift work. Kyoko was obviously restricted but did what she could. Brun spoke to her all the time, she was going to give birth on his ship which would make the child officially Dutch, and he was quite proud of that. He also told her where they were heading and how dangerous it was in that part of the world. She told Tsubo and Obi san some of Brun's horror stories of 'Headhunters and Head Shrinkers', but they just smiled in amusement. The only thing that scared Tsubo was the sea itself, but he still kept that a secret. Obi san had once almost drowned him during his training in a small lake near the town, only pulling him out at the last minute when he realised the boy was in trouble.

He hadn't told anyone about the incident. He was also afraid of deep water.

All was well, they were about a night and a day away from their target Prickly Paradise, when Brun sensed a change in the weather. Indeed he could see the black clouds gathering on the horizon. It shouldn't be a problem; he had ridden out heavy squalls before, and they were so close to their intended target he made the decision to meet it headlong instead of skirting around.

Johan would have gone around.

Brun sent his men up to the rigging to tie up the huge main sails; he ordered the small stay sails to remain for steerage and headed directly for the storm.

The wind rose behind them and began to push them through the ever increasing swell, until the first huge wave smashed into the bow of the 'Charity' flooding the upper deck with water. The helmsman kept her steady, and Brun ordered all non-essential hands to go below deck. Kyoko looked at him worriedly, and he tried to calm her with a look.

Obi san confronted Brun with a look that said, "You are dead if you do, and you are dead if you don't", he had better be right.

Kyoko, Tsubo and Obi san took shelter in Brun's cabin to ride out the storm where her young brother finally admitted to his inability to swim followed by her grandfather's revelation, "Watakushi mo!" – *me neither.* She comforted them by patting her large belly. "If the worst happens, just hold on to me; I have extra buoyancy if you haven't noticed."

The 'Charity' fought on through the night and at first light Brun thought that they had made it until, to his surprise, an Island appeared from the darkness on his Starboard side. His meagre maps had not shown this place and then it suddenly dawned on him, to his horror, he was caught lee side on with the Island; he had condemned everyone to death.

Only he knew that the wind behind him would soon change to beam on, and looking at the tide heading inland towards the land, the 'Charity' would be pushed onto whatever reefs or rocks awaited. He ordered the Main sail be dropped, maybe there would still be a chance that he could fight their way out of their situation. He ordered, "Full a port!" on the rudder and the 'Charity's' bow turned slowly away from the land until a sickening grinding sound came from underneath the hull. They had hit a reef hundred yards from land. A small leak appeared down below and his sailors fought desperately to stem the flow.

Brun spotted a small sandy inlet that the waves were heading towards. His naval brain told him that at the tide was about to turn, so he made his next decision.

"Kyoko! You have to leave the ship, we will come back for you when the storm abates, don't worry; we won't leave you! Head for the sandy beach."

Kyoko couldn't believe what she was hearing but then read the fear in Brun's eyes. Taking hold of Tsubo and Obi san's hands, she leapt into the heavy sea taking both of them with her. Just at that point, the 'Charity' hit the reef once more, so violently that her main sail collapsed to one side of the ship. She was held by the submerged rock while the brave crew attempted to cut away the heavy sails now in the water. Brun looked to see three bobbing heads carried by the tide towards the inlet and then took his last ever swig of rum. This time it didn't taste so good.

A half drowned Tsubo dragged himself up a muddy beach to the cover of a mangrove tree at the edge of a swamp and took cover underneath the spider like branches.

His joy at living was suddenly curtailed when he reached down to his waist to discover the loss of his prized Yashimi.

Looking out to sea he also witnessed the death throes of the 'Charity'.

He imagined the fight that the crew were putting up to save the ship and was saddened to see the whole vessel suddenly flip to Port and disappear beneath the angry waves; taking everyone on-board with her. Due to the sudden change in the tide, anyone else who escaped the ship would be swept out to sea.

He grasped the sharkskin handle of his smaller sword that his own father had forged and presented to him on his 18th birthday, a small comfort.

Remembering the task that had been assigned to him, Tsubo struggled to an upright position. He immediately vomited seawater from his lungs and stomach.

Forcing himself into a steady calm he thought hard with eyes wide open, trying to connect with his lost family.

Recovering slightly he looked West along the shore line where swamp met sandy beach and sure enough, he spotted Obi san and Kyoko at the water's edge, they had also made it to shore. Kyoko had indeed floated them all to safety, albeit short lived. As little as 50 yards away, he resisted the urge to shout out, and stayed hidden under the mangrove roots.

Tsubo's eagle eyes spotted the danger first. 15 natives, black men with hideous white paint on their bodies, most of them carrying small bows with poison tipped arrows, as Brun had told them.

One of them approached the couple waving a stone axe and pointing to the sea, he was an old man, probably as old as his grandfather, "Go back, Go back from where you came from," he appeared to be saying. Tsubo resisted the urge to vomit and stayed under cover. Grasping the handle of his short sword, made ready to move but then the sickness came again. Seawater erupted from his mouth and nose, bile entered his lungs, and he fell into his hiding place silently coughing and gasping for breath. Looking out again he saw ever-loving grandfather bowing gracefully, his sister behind the old man doing the same. The old native lunged at the bowed figure with his axe, but just as he struck, the old man neatly sidestepped, drew his sword and cut of the arm wielding the weapon. Another two natives ran at the old warrior but he cut them down with as many strikes. The remaining natives stepped back and drew their bows. Kyoko took cover behind the old man and drew the small dagger she kept for self-protection, her oversized belly restricting her movement. Tsubo could hear the screams of the injured old native along with the war cries of his compatriots. The first five arrows were easily dealt with by the old man's swift sword. Tsubo took comfort in the display of skill but the pain in his chest and his sick feeling did not ease, this left him still unable to move. He looked on at the small bows used by the natives, his well-trained mind thought they lacked real killing power. Numbers however counted, and soon the natives spread out and chose a second target. Grandfather fended off another dozen arrows before Kyoko was hit in the upper arm. Her scream distracted the old warrior for a second and he was hit in the thigh and then his sword arm which caused him to drop his weapon, a second Yashimi masterpiece. More arrows thudded into the old man's body and eventually he succumbed, kneeling, chanting a life and death mantra he died. Tsubo struggled up, at this point ready to move but heard the final desperate thoughts of Kyoko "Hide little brother! Hide now." With this, she took her dagger and pierced her own heart, falling backwards as if to still protect her unborn child.

Tsubo stayed where he was, hidden to the natives but having to endure the screams of the wounded man, and the other natives who began to laugh at his injury. Tsubo turned his head slightly to witness the next horrors. The tallest of the natives by far picked up the Yashimi sword and with one blow, cut off the head of his beloved grandfather. Picking up the detached head, he waved it into the face of the wounded man, taunting him and making the rest of the Natives laugh louder. He then, almost as an afterthought, turned to the body of Kyoko. Ripping off her kimono, he made two deep cuts, one down and one across her belly, reaching into her womb he took out the unborn baby. After a few moments the screams of the new child rang out to the sounds of the native's song chants that celebrated new birth. And then they left, taking the head of the grandfather, their two dead friends and the new born with them, and of course, the sword.

Tsubouchi Tanaka laid back amongst the legs of the mangrove tree, and one by one removed the thoughts of Horror, then of Sadness and then of Revenge from his mind. He had been given a task and that task was still alive.

He would kill everyone on this Island if he needed to, but first, he must survive, he must learn to live on the Island. After that, he would 'kill them all'.

The ship had ran into the reef at first light and so by this time Tsubo reckoned it to be mid-morning, he had lost a dream, a relic and a family in just a few hours.

"So be it," he concluded, "The way of life, my life, here it begins and here it may end."

"Hajimete imasho." – *Let us begin.*

Tsubo remained in his hiding place, even as the next tide of sea water came into the swamp, his recent training had dictated that.

They must not know I am here was his one and only thought.

He fought off his fear of deep water as the sea was reclaiming its territory. The water began to rise rapidly around his hiding place but still he remained where he was for many hours. The water lapped around his mouth but he refused to leave his position. It was then that he witnessed the last horror.

The small inlet that his sister and grandfather had landed in was now deep with water.

Two menacing tail fins of large bull sharks swam past his hidden position, drawn by the smell of blood. The now floating bodies of his family were dragged under in a flash of surf and then disappeared forever. He would kill them all!

Every now and then he could hear people close to his proximity and thus decided that he would not move until he was completely sure of his own anonymity and that was much later as the sun went down, and the tide ebbed once again.

The first thing he did was take charge of the large crab that had been trying to eat his left testicle for the past hours. One twist with his short sword ensured that he would at least have a meal for that night.

Four or five hours later and after the tide had receded, he found himself sitting in a pool of black mud. The first insect bit into his skin, though he had been conditioned to accept pain, he deemed this unnecessary, and therefore he lavishly covered himself from head to foot including his long thick black hair.

All he had in the world was a silk sash around his middle that carried his short sword and one large crab. The rest of his clothing had been discarded during his fight for life in the sea. Modesty was no longer an issue.

All he could think about at this time was water, he needed to drink. It had rained heavily during the storm so it must have hit this island. Climbing out of the spider like branches of the mangrove tree, he headed to the top of the trunk. Small pools of water still remained captured by the large leaves and he sucked them up generously.

Then he took mud from the ground and mixed this with the largest leaves he could find to create a bowl at the top of the trunk which would gather more water from the next rainfall. He was already thinking about the future.

The insects were incessant in their attack on him but he fought back as much as he could. Every insect that he killed, he ate. That was his training; he was Japanese; he would eat anything. After a while they stopped trying to eat him, or maybe he just got used to it. He journeyed further into the dark swamp, and the deeper he went the safer he felt. His lungs were still bruised by the salt water that he had inhaled and so his monkey like passage across the trees was slow by his normal standards, he could not afford to step onto the soft black mud for fear of leaving tracks, even though he crossed many other footprints in the black molasses that he could just make out in the moonlight.

Often stopping to cough up more mucus; he waited each time for a bird to squeal or a frog to croak to cover his human sound. "They must not know that I am here."

Climbing another of the stumpy spider legged trees he created another well for future, repeating this as he went, drinking the small pools of recent rainwater. Eventually, he reached the end of this swamp where the sea would thunder in, slowed by the spindly legs of the mangrove trees. To his delight, he found a small isolated piece of firm land all on its own. The earth was dry, as dry as the long grass that he sat on as he hacked at the claws of his first prize on this new and strange land. He threw any evidence of his meal into the gentle surf then laid back to sleep for many hours on his own Island in this world.

He awoke to a sound in the distance. A sound that took him by surprise. Women talking. The sounds of the conversations headed towards him but looking down at the new tide beginning to rush in, he doubted they would reach his hiding place. His thoughts were suddenly interrupted by the loud hissing of a snake coiled on a branch to his right, but one effortless swipe with his short sword ensured his next meal. He listened intently to the chatter and counted as many as eight different voices. Were these the mature women of the Island? He calculated that with men and children, there could be up to forty natives living here, so he would kill them all.

He silently chewed on the raw snake and waited until the voices of the women departed and then spent the rest of the day moving around 'his' swamp. The perfect hiding place he deemed, no man would venture into this place without fear.

As the new tide rushed in, he moved back into the heart of the swamp, cautiously moving across the trees, and the spindly legs of the mangrove, leaving no sign. Racing the sea to reach the area where the women had been gathering, he looked down at the places they had 'worked' in. Part of a black shell protruded from the mud, one they had left for later. Tsubo pried the large mud clam from its home and opened the feast with a twist of his short sword. He ate the contents before re-dressing himself in black mud and finding a suitable hiding place for the next day, taking care to hide the empty shell, evidence of his small meal.

The next morning women appeared, chattering. *Good, no suspicion*, he felt confident in his ability to make himself look a part of the tree that he was within. Their men had killed and it was good, everyone was happy again. No foreign contamination of their Island – good. Tsubo watched as they worked; he saw what they gathered and how. For one whole week he observed. Every day, as the tide changed, the women left and Tsubo hurried to gather what he could before the oncoming tide claimed the earth.

He lived well on mud clams, small crab and everything else that moved. To him, this was a feast. They came and went each day, came and went and all the time Tsubo observed from his hideouts. He changed trees all the time, making himself look part of them, getting closer and closer to their gatherings guessing where they would be the next day until eventually he could hear everything they were saying. Even though he could not understand their strange language, he could recognise their fears, and they started to fear.

As they would normally look down all the time as they were gathering, now, every so often, they would look up, as if they knew they were being watched. This thought was compounded by the arrival of men.

One day, five natives appeared covered in patchy white paint, four of them carrying their small bows. They shouted loudly and fired their weapons blindly into the surrounding trees. Tsubo remained hidden but bemused.

An old man with the group held a bowl of earth in his one arm, the other stump still dressed from a recent wound. One of the younger natives held the clay bowl for him as the he picked up handfuls of earth to throw around the area Shouting and chanting. At the end of the old man's rant was a musical chant that all the other men joined in with before they drew their bows and fired off many more arrows. Tsubo resisted the option to smile as it might crack the dried mud that he had camouflaged himself with. At one point in the proceedings he was in touching distance of his aggressors. The desire to laugh out loud was very strong but once again, training took over. He would kill them all, later.

They began to sing their healing chant again but loudly and in great harmony. Tsubo was impressed at this sound and another thought prevailed. He was being entertained, he was the main character in the Kabuki play, they were the chorus, he did not want this symphony to end, but as it did, he realised,

"Kono hitotachi o shirite imasu." – *They know I am here.*

"Hajimete ho ga ii desu." – *I will have to begin.*

Hours later, when the whole cavalcade of people had left the area, he gathered all the spent arrows that he could find. He held the first arrow tip to his nose, he smelt a pungent unfamiliar odour, poison. They really did know that he was here.

Food was good in the swamp, many mud clams and decent sizes crabs from his woven traps when he could afford bait. Tsubo had no idea how large or how small an area this Island actually was. Three weeks living in a swamp had become quite claustrophobic, his dark olive skin was starting to turn pail and now he needed to venture out.

Also, he needed water, it had not rained for a full week, and his store in the various trees was becoming bracken. At first he cautiously followed the tracks of the women at night, by the light of the moon and stars. They always led him to that point where his sister and grandfather had met their end. This was as far as he could safely go without leaving tracks, as a sandy causeway led the way for about a hundred yards leading up to a hillside path. On this night he took his chance. Tsubo bowed in respect to his family before sprinting across the open ground using the old tracks he eventually made cover.

Waiting, listening, nerves stretched and he eventually moved again. Stealthily moving up the hilly track yard by yard, he reached a point where the direction split into two choices. Tsubo took cover and waited. It was then that he heard the sound, a small trickle of water somewhere near, he could hear it, smell it.

Stealthily, following all his instincts he moved towards the water, a small stream creating a pool at the bottom of the hill and off the path.

Just as he thought, the natural well was being guarded but not very well. There were two young boys, probably his own age but possibly lacking in skill.

He waited for at least one more hour, watching their movement in these early hours.

There were indeed only two and one was very much asleep. The other, however badly disguised, was at least trying to do his job. He was quite a fat young boy, Tsubo observed, the rest of this Island must be full of food according to this theory.

The young man wanted to relieve himself, Tsubo had noticed his agitation and body language, now he could wait no more and stood up from his guarding spot to pee.

Tsubo moved, and positioned himself an arm's throw behind the young warrior in absolute silence. Just before the young native had finished his business, he instinctively felt Tsubo's presence. As he turned, his eyes opened wide at the grey ghostly sight in front of him.

As he did so, Tsubo jabbed two fingers into his eye sockets from his right hand, not hard enough to blind the young man permanently, just enough to bruise them temporarily. As the young man screamed, his friend awoke swiftly and suffered the same blow from Tsubo's left hand as he stood. Before they could react with any of their primitive weapons, Tsubo grabbed them both by the back of the neck and slammed the two foreheads together. They both slumped to the ground as one. Unconscious for the next twenty minutes.

Tsubo filled his belly with the fresh water. This may be his last drink he thought, the killing starts soon. He suddenly realised his natural change in attitude, then corrected himself.

"I will kill men, not boys." Then he hid.

Sure enough at about the time he'd thought, the women appeared on the pathway. He heard them coming... They found the boys first.

Both temporary blinded and ranting about ghosts. Tsubo smiled when the elder woman smacked the boys with her sharp digging stick and sent them home with a young girl who guided them up the hill towards their village. Tsubo noted how tall she was compared to the rest of the natives and how gentle she was with the two boy warriors. The elder woman looked around suspiciously. He was fifteen feet away from her, but he knew she couldn't see him.

The women headed towards the swamp, Tsubo followed the path upward. Just a little way along the track he spotted a tree with cones containing black seeds. He had seen the native women in the swamp snacking on these and felt sure they were safe to consume. Quickly picking a generous handful he found cover before carefully picking the skin from the first nut.

Chewing on the fingernail-sized white fruit gave him a renewed sense of hope, He could survive. For a short time at least. One meal at a time, he thought to himself, and he could learn more, much more from these people, before he killed them.

He had decided he would need a boat. The water was infested with large sharks as he knew well. To confirm this, he had watched as some of the natives in their double float canoes were diving a little way out from the shore. At least two canoes were on guard at a time, on the lookout for the beasts.

Shouts went up as soon as a tail fin was spotted and others beat the water ferociously to warn the submerged divers.

This was the only time in the three weeks spent in the swamp that he had witnessed the natives leaving the boat to dive into the water. Normally they were afloat hunting for large fish and even sharks themselves. There must have been something very precious down there.

Once he saw them struggle with a huge bull shark that was as long as one of their canoes. They landed in the small bay next to the swamp and it took three of the natives to carry the feast. The canoe was left alone and unguarded on the beach but Tsubo just looked on, his plan was not complete.

He could, and would, learn a lot from these people, before he killed them.

Instinct headed Tsubo across the other side of the Island, The canoes had to be somewhere in one location and he must find this place. A few hours of stealthy movement rewarded his thought. Looking down onto a sweeping sandy bay, there were fifteen canoes upon the shore and two more were heading out to sea through the surf. He watched their rowing technique as they cut through the 10 feet waves. Tsubo thought to himself,

"Every battle has a structure, first plan the structure, then add the element of luck." Words that his grandfather had spoken to him as a young boy in training. At the time it did not mean a thing, but, now he understood. Then he headed back to the swamp as the rain teemed down. He would not need their water source again.

The weather was bad this day as Tsubo observed the canoes returning to shore. As usual, the greeting party on the beach was large but then depleted as every canoe returned with its wares.

Out to sea, Tsubo noticed one very small dot on the horizon struggling to return home. Reading the waves and the wind he realised that it would not make it home to this beach, and so took the gamble on where it would go next.

It was at least an hour before dark but he would have to move now to be in place. The women would have left the swamp and be back at the village by now, he was sure.

Standing upright, he was suddenly aware of his appearance. Five feet two inches tall, slim muscular build, and covered from head to foot in dried mud which gave him a ghostly grey appearance. Perhaps this really was the colour of war. The colour of death.

Tsubo ran, ran as fast as he could, he wanted to be in place and be ready. Reaching the swamp in minutes he began to prepare. His now well-worn silk cloth was hidden in a safe place, totally naked and covered in fresh black swamp mud. On his knees he prayed a silent mantra of life & death and as dark settled, buried himself in the sand at the point where he knew the canoe would land.

One hour later the canoe arrived exactly at the spot that Tsubo himself had predicted. Through the inch of sand around his ears he could hear the efforts of two natives hauling the canoe up to safety, shouting to each other in exhausted tones. One pushed and one pulled, then suddenly the one pulling fell backwards, tripped by something in the sand.

The blade of the small sword held by Tsubo entered at the back of the neck and finished halfway thru the natives windpipe.

The second native concerned at his friends silence rushed to his assistance. As he bent to examine his friend, Tsubo's right hand leapt from the sand to grab the back of the natives head and at the same time thrust the blade through the first windpipe into the second one. Tsubo held tight until the struggling stopped.

He then pushed at the limp bodies and withdrew his sword.

He now stood covered in a cocktail of black swamp mud, sand and now blood. Quickly he dragged the bodies to the water's edge and then set about dragging the canoe back into the water. Blood oozed into the sea turning the surf a deep red in the fading light.

With a little effort, he threw the bodies into the canoe and pushed the boat out to sea in the small inlet. His chosen destination was at the edge of the swamp where it would be possible to hide his stolen vessel. The incoming tide would cover the evidence of his small slaughter and hopefully assist in the mooring of the canoe.

Furiously he paddled facing the incoming tide until he reached the edge of the long mangrove roots obstructing the boats movement and he had to repeatedly push out to sea to make any headway.

Finally he cleared the small inlet and headed the corner towards his hiding place. Looking down at his own bare feet, he found them swimming in blood and seawater as the canoe was not completely watertight, looking behind he suddenly realised that the boat was trailing an irresistible flow of blood made evident by the two menacing tailfins following closely behind.

The two sharks attacked as one, coming right up to the flimsy sides of the canoe.

Tsubo whacked at them with his paddle but they persisted, threatening to bite the whole boat to pieces. Looking at his two dead passengers he chastised himself for being so stupid. Kneeling in the bottom of the canoe to maintain balance, he lifted the first corpse over the side which was grabbed by one of the sharks even before it had entered the water.

Tsubo quickly deposited the other body into the sea and paddled on, easier now due the loss of weight. At last he reached his intended destination and after a bit of hacking with his short sword, managed to conceal his new prize in the mangrove swamp alongside his one-man inner island.

Only then could he stop for a moment to retain his composure. Sitting cross-legged on the seat of the canoe, wondering how he had conquered his fear of deep water, he closed his eyes and calmed as his training had taught him, hearing Obi san's wise words.

"Fear in your mind is not fear, it is just a distraction, if you concentrate on 'your task', you will not be distracted; you will have no fear."

With their joint fear of deep water, Tsubo had discarded this comment but now it came back to him from the depths of his memory.

"Now, I am not afraid of anything."

Suddenly his eyes snapped open in the fading light and landed on a package stored at the front of the canoe, a vine wrapped bundle that he carefully pulled apart to reveal a recently killed small pig.

This was turning out to be a successful day he thought to himself as he cut away small slivers of raw meat with his razor sharp sword and chewed slowly on this excellent feast.

Tsubo pondered over the danger of gorging on this small beast full of succulent meat and decided to only eat enough to replete his hungry mind.

Other booty was stashed in the front of the canoe, two small bows and a dozen arrows. Tsubo sniffed the tips of the ordinance – the same acrid smell from his other stash, poison.

He held the bows, caressing and sniffing at the wood, remembering the texture, the precise location of its source.

He would make a bow, removing the taut strings he put the two lengths of wood together, designing the new weapon, it would be much more powerful than the ones he held in his hand. He thought about his favourite bow that he had left at Shimabara Castle before saying goodbye to his father, thinking that he would never have use for this weapon again, how wrong had he been.

Then at the very bottom of the small Boat, hidden under a large palm leaf found two newly decapitated heads alongside the primitive sword that must have been used to despatch them.

He picked up the piece of iron and felt disgust in the poor workmanship that had gone into this weapon of death. At least in his country you would have the dignity of being beheaded with a respectful blade.

He guessed the heads at one time belonged to a couple of men, just a little older than himself and admired the red coloured adornments in their long black hair. This he could just make out in the last moments of the sun.

Sitting upright and cross-legged on the bridge of this newly pirated prize, he slept a long satisfying sleep, dreaming about the bow.

Tsubo awoke with a chill for the first time in two weeks; the weather must be changing for the worse, or maybe, there was another storm in the air.

Taking a small meal from the pig he set about preparing the small beast for preservation.

The young animal was whole and had to be cleaned but he would waste nothing. His crab traps had long waited for some decent bait, so the offal of the pig would serve this course and he wondered to himself, *would he ever need them again?'*.

The back legs would be hung to dry in a safe hideaway, his strict routine of the past few weeks made him do this.

Tsubo peered out from the edge of the mangrove. Three natives were studying the ground at his point of slaughter; the place where his grandfather and sister had been mercilessly killed. They shouted amongst themselves, two pointed to the sea but one insisted on the sand. Tsubo looked on impassively, feeling boosted by his first kill. It would not be his last.

He could have demised all with just his short sword but he just waited patiently. All he needed from them were tracks to cover his as they made their way back to their village, oh and as a matter of fact, one more native bow or the equivalent in wood.

He would make a composite bow, three of theirs into one of his. A superior weapon. He had witnessed the suspicion of the native pointing to the ground and realised that the tide did not take every bit of evidence from the killing sand and tried hard to realise his mistake. Self-castigation over, he followed the three along the causeway, to the hill path and then upward at the fork in the trail.

They stopped for a short time to speak to the 'men' guarding the fresh water source.

Tsubo listed to the alien conversation for a while, trying to understand the inference in their dialogue. Minutes later, the meeting finished and the three headed off towards the village.

This particular trail led to the highest point on the island. Tsubo stopped here and hid as only he knew how, feeling the trees and the undergrowth around him. A spider's web caught his left hand, Tsubo waited until his fingers were attacked by the insect and then swooped with his right, pinched the head and then ate the body. A nice snack, he was becoming one with the island.

Moving to the next cover, he felt the branches, straight upright, strong and pliable. This was the source of the bow. He let his feelings run riot as he held each upward branch in turn and finally picked the most suitable pieces.

Ten silent cuts with his sword secured the prize which he held in both hands, sniffing the wood and sap, put to one side to be gathered on his journey back to the swamp, a place he now thought of as home.

And then he smelled the smell. A sweet sickly human smell, his first impressions were, that they should not be here, he thought about how he would deal with this back in Japan.

I will recover; I will recover to purify your island gods.

"Kono shima wa sugoi da ne?" – *This Island is wonderful, isn't it?*

"Iru o shirite imasu." – *I know why am I here.*

"Atarashi Nippon ni o tsukeimasu." – *I will make the New Japan here!*

And with a silent thought said to himself, "Gambatteru." – *I will do my best.*

Now he wanted to kill again. The desire was beginning to become stronger. He fought between task and want. Task and desire, task took over.

Tsubo knew that when he braced the top of the hill he would come to the village, the place where all his prospective victims lived. He must use calm, use his training.

Tsubo took his first look at the village from his vantage point, and from where he was there did not appear to be much of a plan to the small living area, just many mud and leaf houses scattered about on different levels.

His analytic brain began planning routes between the various structures. Two more visual angles would make his reconnoitre complete.

Containing his bloodlust, he moved off the track and made stealth into the undergrowth heading to the high side of the village. All the time he smelt the smell, cooking, and just people in general. Finally he reached a second point where he looked down onto the target.

It was so different from his first option and as the tall native moved from the large middle hut, Tsubo realised that this was all he needed to see.

One hour later, after gathering his hidden stash of branches, he was sitting on his boat carving wood and feasting on raw meat. For this night and this night alone he would make a fire.

For hours he worked quickly and eventually ended with three parts of a bow that fitted perfectly together. Striking a piece of flint with his short sword, he ignited the tinder and gradually added small pieces of branch until he created a small but hot blaze. On a flat piece of wood he offered the tree resin that he had gathered.

The objects fizzled and melted into a mix that he stirred with a small branch. He resisted the temptation to cook some of his prized pig, but anyway, Tsubo had been raised on a diet of raw fish & meat and this would only be a western luxury as he called it.

The glue was ready. Carefully he added the melted resin to the wood and bound them tightly with the thin strands of tree bark taken from the same copse. The weapon seemed solid but only time would tell. He put the long bow to one side and began to concentrate on the bowstring. He had two shorter strings from the original native bows but these were just one length of tough tree bark. He would need to braid a longer string but the thickness of the bark made this impractical, some thinner, stronger material was required. He looked down to the bottom of the canoe where one of the decapitated heads stared up at him with dead eyes.

Tsubo smiled back before cutting off a large chunk of long black hair from one of the Heads, discarding the red coloured leaves woven into the matted wool.

He painstakingly cut the two original bowstrings in half before platting the bark and human hair together to form an incredibly strong and longbow string.

He guessed the length that the string should be and finished the plait with a circle at either end. These would fit into the carefully carved notches of the new bow but not yet. The Bow makers in his family would spend as much as three months making such a weapon. Tsubo had but a few hours. Finally he worked on 'his' arrows. He had already gathered at least thirty of the islanders failed shots. Not all of their tips had been coated in poison. Tsubo took off about twenty of their crude but effective flint tips and transferred them to his own design, longer, straighter and with birds feather's, gathered from 'his' swamp, attached with the help of melted tree resin and human hair.

His daily observation of the tide determined his next moment of action. The sea rode east to west and with this Tsubo pushed his boat out towards the surf.

Rowing gently, because he knew the strong tide was taking him; he rounded the corner of the island in his stolen canoe. The surf rose furiously trying to push him back, but then he fought himself into the large bay.

From a hundred yards out the native on the beach looked up to see the apparition of Tsubo standing up, a body covered in swamp mud, gradually drying that gave a black and grey appearance – 'The Ghost'.

It must have been a small but terrifying sight. He held two decapitated heads in his hands, lifting them up in sign of triumph, saying nothing. Ghosts and Ninja's do not make noise.

The native ran back towards the village screaming and then returned a few minutes later with what seemed like the whole island's warrior population.

They all chanted as one, the same chant he had heard the first day on the island, the day his sister and grandfather died. Any thought of sympathy for man woman or child left his mind.

Tsubo took care to stay out of range of the natives arrows using the paddle, taunting them and all shots fell short of his boat until finally he felt the change in the tide. The natives also knew this and went to their canoes to launch.

Tsubo picked up his new bow, quickly attached the string for the first time and fitted the first arrow. Somebody shouted a warning and Tsubo shot the shaft into the middle of that native's chest.

He then rained down accurate fire on those attempting to float their canoes. The plan worked, the natives took cover from his murderous fire and he stopped when only two arrows remained.

Quickly he put down the bow and started to paddle furiously out to sea. When the islanders realised Tsubo had put himself out of range they quickly resumed launching their boats for the chase.

Tsubo smiled to himself looking back at his foe, but then as he turned to continue his plan something caught his eye.

There were two, no, three large sea going canoes far in the distance, each boat carried at least ten rowers who were heading directly towards his Island. He could make out flashes of Red on the heads of the attackers.

He stopped for a moment and realised that they were heading in the direction of the bay. Looking back to the beach, the natives also recognised this, and had aborted their chase for him. A bigger threat was on the horizon.

A serious worry clouded his accurate thoughts, this was not part of the plan, and it annoyed him, but he would recover the situation, and still had confidence. This was to be his day of triumph, or day of death. "Let them come on," he said, "I will kill them all."

He let the first sea going canoe get within 100 yards and stood challenging this new threat. The sea however began to bounce his canoe around so he could not stand and shoot any more.

Tsubo decided to revert to his original plan.

"It doesn't matter, I will kill even more of them."

Paddling furiously for 30 minutes his general like mind recalculated the plan over and over again. Because of his accuracy with the bow, the Island natives would be outnumbered if this was indeed an attack by rival warriors, and by now he could see the vivid red colour in the hair of the approaching warriors. "I will recover, I will succeed," he sang to himself.

Meanwhile, the natives on the beach started to organise themselves, guided by the tall chief. This was the last thing that Tsubo noticed as he rounded the corner of the island.

Tsubo landed at the small inlet near the swamp, quickly bowing to the memories of his sister and grandfather. Not even bothering to secure the boat, he rushed, caution to the wind, in the direction of the village arriving at his first point in as little as 8 minutes.

Only waiting for a few moments, he confirmed his first impression, the village was deserted. The women had left to hide with the children.

Quickly he headed for the large hut in the middle of the compound. There was no need for caution now. In the distance he heard shouts and screams, the sound of a battle.

Calling on calm he entered the hut, feeling the reef mat underneath his bare feet, the first man made surface he felt in almost one month. He closed his eyes and felt for the sword, asked it to call to him. Turning about sharply to his surprise and delight were two Yashimi swords, hung trophy like above the entrance of the doorway. His mind went back to the Natives diving in the shark-infested water – 'there must have been something very precious down there.'

Alongside the swords were many shrunken, hairy heads, the last of which he recognised as his beloved grandfather.

Tsubo then bowed deeply. "Obi San. Dozo, I rara ra shimasu. Tsubo." – *Grandfather, I am here.*

Drawing the swords from their sheaths, which he gently placed against the thin wall of the hut, he held the blades upright with two hands, the blunt sides of the beasts gently bumping against his forehead as he recited a silent mantra:

94

one that his father had taught him. Now holding two Yashimi's, he was going to be unstoppable.

And then he was moving fast out of the hut towards the beach. Stopping before the edge of the huts, he peered a corner and witnessed two Red coloured men binding the hands of one of the islanders. They had colourful painted faces and red coloured leaves woven into their long black hair, unlike the white war paint of his island's natives.

This thought went straight to his heart for a split second and he paused, Yashimi swords held low.

The two Red coloured warriors were transfixed at the sight of Tsubo. As well as being covered from head to feet in grey dried mud, he was completely naked apart from a silk belt that carried his small sword. By the petrified look in their eyes he must be a ghost. He held their gaze for a few seconds and then moved.

Tsubo's first blow took off the head and right arm of the red painted native on the left, then spinning round obliterated the head of the other native with the second Yashimi.

Both bodies fell simultaneously, such was the speed of the attack and left the terrified islander standing with hands still tied behind his back. Tsubo recognised him, a short little boy with a fat belly now shaking with fear. Tsubo indicated to him to turn around. He did so and Tsubo cut his bonds, one second later the native turned around free and the Ninja was nowhere in sight.

Tsubo ran downwards towards the beach, he noticed the sun directly in his eyes, he would use this.

Five more red coloured warriors were heading for the village and they had the misfortune of meeting Tsubo on the path. He killed the first four with a pattern of, slash, stab, slash stab, and with the fifth, he crossed swords and decapitated the man with a 'swish' sound of the two blades running together.

Tsubo's blood lust was in full flow, his confidence was running high now. He would succeed. He cleaned the blood from his two Yashimis using the loincloths of the natives that he had just killed and walked slowly downhill.

On the beach an artillery battle was occurring. The island natives were huddled around their boats firing arrows towards the red warriors camped in a rock outcrop the other side of the inlet, barely 50 yards apart, such was the range of their small bows.

Tsubo walked directly into the middle of the barrage, holding the Yashimis resting on his left and right shoulders, each highly polished blade firing bright sunshine blinding the eyes of both sides.

They all stopped firing, blinded by the reflected sunlight and looked on at this strange sight protecting their eyes from the fierce gleam.

A long tense pause took place as Tsubo stood still impassively.

The tall chief of the island natives stood and shouted to the opposing side.

"We know this ghost, our ancestors have said he is one of us. He has lived on our land. He can even become one with us!"

The rest of the island warriors backed up these words with a musical chant, "He is one with us, he is one of us, he is one with this island."

Tsubo did not understand a word of the dialog but at this last musical statement an aggressive roar went up from the red warrior side, this was his cue, one small turn of the Yashimis shone all the brilliant light of the sun into the eyes of the invaders, blinding their aim.

Tsubo moved purposefully across the sand towards the rocks and watched as poisoned arrows fell all around him. Thirty yards, twenty yards, and then he ran, reaching the first large rock in a few seconds and cut down his first victim straight across his belly as he leant back to avoid an arrow.

Two more red natives fired their arrows at point blank range but he cut both shafts with small flicks of his swords before he dispatched them.

Another volley headed in his direction but he back flipped onto the top of the rock and down the other side directly behind three other warriors who had left their positions.

He slashed left and then right with the Yashimis, then sensed more attackers coming behind him, stabbed two natives native through their hearts with a double reverse thrust.

Fending off another barrage of arrows, cutting each one with swift cuts from the precious swords, he ran at the red adorned natives in his path. There were at least eight of them, and after he had cut down the first two, the others had no more stomach for a fight. These and other survivors ran for their canoes but were one by one slaughtered by the island natives.

Tsubo watched as they dispatched their enemies. He felt elated, light headed even, his' blood lust had been sated.

Walking out from behind the rock, he surprised himself at his unsteady walk, confused slightly, he stopped, swords held low.

He stared at the Island natives who stared back completely motionless, then turning his head to the side, noticed for the first time three shafts protruding from the back of his left shoulder blade.

Collapsing to his knees he began to pray the same death mantra that his dear grandfather had recited almost a month before. Panic took over as he completely forgot the poem. He tried to remember the 'Hiku' but it was useless.

The last thing he recalled on that day was the tall native speaking close to his face before picking him up from the sand and carrying him in his arms.

Tsubo awoke from a long bad dream, his first sense smelled something familiar; it was that hut; the big hut where the floor felt so good. A hand caressed his forehead, a strong hand, his vision was blurred and he felt his own body, so weak. After a few moments, he saw clearly, then he saw his helper for the first time, it was an old man with only one arm, murmuring chants, touching him, putting water into his mouth, it tasted bitter.

Only then did he know that he was still alive. His right arm moved to grasp a weapon but it was not there, frustration built as the man with one arm laughed. The man's mouth opened to the biggest smile hat Tsubo had ever seen, most of his teeth were missing, and he reminded him of a hideous doll he had possessed as a child. He fell into a restless sleep, surrounded by nightmares of that small china clay figure.

The next time he awoke it was in the middle of the night. The moon was incredibly bright so he could make out shapes in the hut. On the floor sleeping in front of him was a long figure, covered in a thin cloth blanket.

He felt the skirt of cut palm leaves that had been attached to his silk belt to cover his modesty. The Natives had cleaned him of dried mud and he no longer felt the itchy

Sensation of this dressing.

Managing to lift and turn his head slightly he saw another image, sitting upright, holding a small bundle.

He heard sucking sounds, a baby feeding, and then he stared into two large eyes, glinting in the moonlight. Their eyes met in the dark and after a few moments she stopped her function and brought the baby to him. Struggling to lift himself even more, he gazed upon the new child, a boy.

In the bright moonlight he could make out the colour of the skin. Much lighter that the natives, and even whiter that his own. This was to be expected he thought, even so, the child still retained the slanted eyes of a southern Asian and he even saw something of himself in the face. After all, this was his nephew. Tsubo slipped into unconsciousness once again and slept.

He was no longer a threat to the villagers, more of a fascination. Every day he was expected to die but kept defying death. The poison was bacterial. It attacked the main organs and as fate would have it, the only reason the child was alive was because Kyoko had stabbed her own heart and so stopping the poison from reaching the baby in the womb, so even if he did somehow recover, there was no guarantee that he would ever be the same again.

One day he awoke and his head was clear, the ever-attentive one-armed old man rushed outside and returned with a steaming bowl of soup.

Tsubo took the wooden spoon himself and gratefully thanked the old man with his eyes before taking a sip of the warm liquid. A wry smile came over his lips, this was green turtle soup, a dish that his Royal family in Japan would share on special occasions.

An overwhelming sense of 'homesickness' threatened to make him weep, but that would not be correct for a young Samurai trained in the art of 'Ningitsu'.

The old man left him to feed himself and left the hut, Tsubo heard excited conversation outside.

Struggling with the pain that still wracked his whole body, he managed to sit up on the reef mat, and looked down surprised to see three swords laid by his side.

Two precious Yashimi and his own short sword. Gradually he stood up with the help of one Yashimi before silently taking it from its sheath.

Outside the men were gathered. Sitting in a circle talking insistently, that was until they saw Tsubo standing at the entrance of the hut, unsteady but still holding one precious sword. They were alarmed and all stood, but this was not what he wanted anymore.

The tall Chief knew this and stood unarmed in front of Tsubo, well within sword range.

Tsubo then placed the tip of the sword in the sand and began to draw.

He drew the shape of a large ship. Two tall masts with large sails.

Then at the back of the picture he drew a flag, a simple shape, three rectangles together that formed a square. Pointing to the first rectangle he lifted the sword towards a Red flowered bush, the third he picked out a Blue bush, and the middle he gently rubbed the end of the sword onto the belly of the chief across some white paint.

The tall chief nodded in understanding. Tsubo in return bowed as low as he could without falling forwards. Tsubo then handed his sword to the Chief who helped him back onto his bed of reef.

***

Tsubo awoke to a new sensation, the feeling of motion on the sea. He looked up to see the Chief sitting alongside his daughter. She must be, the faces are so similar.

She cradled the child under her cloak. The rest of the natives paddled their large canoe in such unison that he felt the surge forward at each stroke. Every so often the chief would give him sips of water from an earthen jar that contained the healing herbs for his condition. After a while he felt good enough to sit up in the boat and experience the sea journey, he amazed himself at his lack of fear from being in deep water, in fact, he began to enjoy the experience. The waves sent small raindrops of wetted salt that he occasionally licked from his lips. The Tall chief did the same as he, and Tsubo created some sort of bond together with occasional eye contact.

Then he looked towards the daughter, probably his own age, maybe younger, she held his stare for a while with her big brown eyes, the same stare they had held in the hut, but then she fussed about her charge.

The land appeared on the horizon at the same time as the sea calmed.

The natives seemed to know this already, after navigating their way around a deadly reef, they entered a large bay.

Tsubo knew the ship immediately; he had seen it many times before: 'The Batavia'.

Other local canoes were surrounding the vessel, all trading one thing or another. Every island village seemed to be converging on this one small floated island. As they approached the large sea-going vessel, Tsubo indicated that he needed to stand. The crew helped, mostly the short one with the fat belly, until he was fully upright and then he shouted to the ship.

"JOHAN SAN, TSUBO TANAKA!"

The ships company were immediately ordered into action. All other trading canoes were ordered away at gunpoint. Tsubo grasped the wrist of the tall chief as he regained a sitting position and shook his head, coughing loudly into his own palm showed him a blood stain in the mucus.

Tsubo beckoned the chief to help him into a kneeling position so he could shout once again. But he didn't have to.

"TSUBO KYOKO!"

The familiar voice from the ship shouted down to the large canoe. It was Joseph. Tsubo collapsed at the sound of his beloved sister's name being called out loudly, in his eyes, he had failed. The tall chief held on to him tightly as he coughed more blood from his lungs.

Johan looked over the side but could not see the canoe due to the rounded girth of the 'Batavia'.

"Tsubo Kyoko!" Joseph shouted again. "Joseph, lower the cradle," Johan mumbled from his still broken face.

The ship's cradle lowered down towards the canoe, picked up its passengers and then lifted them towards the upper deck.

Johan waited with anticipation as the cradle rose and finally reached its destination.

Inside the cradle sat a tall native girl nurturing a young baby, a long wrapped package leant by her side.

Johan rushed to the side of his ship and looked down. He saw nothing else below him but blue water.

Johan began crying for only the second time in twenty-eight years and then walked towards the native girl, who Joseph had helped onto the ship's deck.

She held the baby towards him and simply said, "Boy."

Johan held his son in his arms for the first time and cried further until Joseph quietly requested.

"Orders, sir?"

"Kaerimasho, Joseph." – *Let's go home*.

The End.